AN AUCTION OF SECRETS

A COTSWOLD ANTIQUE MYSTERY

VICTORIA TAIT

KANGA PRESS

Cover Design by Daniela Colleo of StunningBookCovers.com
Editing Allie Douglas

For more information visit VictoriaTait.com

CHAPTER ONE

DOTTY

Akemans auction room had an air of tired neglect, like a village fête after the bunting had come down, leaving only echoes of laughter and distant chatter.

Thirty-one-year-old Dotty Sayers surveyed the open space, her shoulders sagging as her gaze lingered on the ink-blot stain of winter water damage on the high ceiling and the mottling of black, brown, and yellow on the once-white walls.

Without the clamour of bidders, the careful display of furniture, and the warm glow of strategic lighting, the room's flaws were exposed.

"Never mind," said the always professional and neatly dressed Marion Rook, handing Dotty a mug of steaming tea. It was Darjeeling, and its delicate floral notes offered some comfort to her troubled thoughts.

The grey-haired Marion favoured coffee, its rich aroma of cardamom masking the musty undertones of the room.

"At least the country house sale at Marchwood Hall was a success," Marion continued. "I spoke to several of our regular customers. They're concerned, of course, what with the newspaper allegations of impropriety, Georgina's sudden resignation, and your appointment as manager. But I reassured them that it's business as usual."

"Not that usual," Dotty replied, rubbing the toe of her boot against the worn nylon carpet. "Since we've had to combine this month's meagre sale entries with Amanda's April sale at Cirencester Auctioneers."

"We had plenty of lots in the March sale, and I've already had an enquiry for a house clearance in Westonbirt. I'm sure May will be better. Now the trees are blossoming and the hedgerows are returning to life, so are the people of the Cotswolds. They love nothing better than a spring clean and a clear-out."

"I thought you said they love nothing better than a good gossip," Dotty said with a sigh.

She knew Marion was trying to lift her spirits, but the creeping sense of uncertainty was hard to ignore.

She'd first walked through Akemans' front door three and a half years ago. Gilly Wimsey, who ran Akemans antique centre, had offered her a job as the auction receptionist.

The role included compiling the monthly sales catalogues and, as she worked, she learned more about antiques. Enough for her to undertake her own commissions for private clients the previous summer.

And now she was back in the Cotswolds. The rolling hills, the quaint villages, and the honey-coloured stone cottages were dear to her, as were many of the eccentric characters she called friends.

But had she made a mistake accepting the role of auction manager? She'd been so grateful and proud to take it on, believing it was her chance to make something of herself. Yet now, standing in the cold, empty, auction room, the weight of its problems pressed heavily on her.

Akemans was charming in its way, but it felt stuck in the past. Other auction houses had moved on, with sleek purpose-built facilities. Akemans still expected bidders to sit on the very furniture being sold.

They did have an online platform, but they weren't matching the seamless presentation and efficiency of their competitors.

And why was Marmaduke, the head of the family business, still so reluctant to acknowledge her position as auction manager?

"Everyone loves a good gossip," Marion said with a quick smile, drawing Dotty out of her introspection.

The telephone rang in the reception and office area at the front of the building.

"Perhaps that's a new client with a collection of Chippendale furniture to sell," Marion said in a light and positive tone as she turned and strode purposefully across the auction room.

The door opened, and Zach stepped back allowing Marion to pass before he entered. His tall, athletic frame moved easily through the space as he approached Dotty.

"Gilly's in denial," he said in his American accent, his tone regretful as he ran his hand through his short dark hair.

"I told her about the cracks in the shared wall between this building and the antique centre, but she brushed me off. Said the flour mill had stood for over a hundred and fifty years before her father converted it, and the stone walls were solid."

Dotty looked at him fondly and replied, "Building maintenance isn't her priority, not after the thefts last month in the antique centre. Several stallholders are refusing to pay their rent unless she installs CCTV cameras."

"I tried to talk to her about that too, but she said it'll have to wait. There's just no money, not after footfall slowed in the antique centre, and the cancelling of two auctions already this year."

Dotty looked at Zach, clutching one hand with the other, and asked, "Do you think I made a mistake accepting this position?

"You didn't exactly have a choice, and you couldn't have known about all the problems. But just look around." Zach turned in a circle, gesturing with his arms. "All this space."

"But what do we do with it?"

"I'm not sure, but there has to be a viable opportunity."

"Good news," Marion said as she entered and crossed the auction room, her tortoiseshell-framed glasses bouncing against one of the gold buttons of her poppy red cardigan on their black cord.

Dotty ran a hand through her bobbed, blonde highlighted hair as she waited for Marion to continue.

"That was a new client asking if we can deal with the contents of a house in Kingham. It belonged to his recently deceased uncle."

"There you are," Zach said, smiling optimistically. "Even death brings new opportunities."

CHAPTER TWO

DOTTY

Two days later, Dotty drove her compact but surprisingly nippy Audi A1 north along a ridge road from the Cotswold town of Burford, carefully avoiding puddles left by the overnight rain.

April was known for its heavy showers, but the clouds had cleared, and the morning sunlight warmed her face through the windscreen.

She felt lighter and freer after the confines and problems of the auction house. And her mood was tinged with excitement, as this was a part of the job she loved. Visiting other people's homes and uncovering treasures they had hidden away.

But sometimes it also brought a quiet sadness that someone's lifetime accumulation could be discarded, their treasured possessions dismissed as worthless. And that the stories and memories of those items were lost with the person who had cherished them.

Her destination was the secluded village of Kingham, which she'd never visited before. Following the instructions on her phone, she turned right onto a narrow single-track lane.

She loved the changing English seasons, but spring was her favourite, bringing new life after the dark cold winter months. Slowing for a bend in the road, she noticed a periphery of yellow flowers. Clusters of late-flowering daffodils stood tall among primroses, cowslips and the waxy petals of lesser celandines.

The previous day, their new client, Tim Reynolds, had dropped off the keys at Akemans for his uncle's cottage in the village.

Marion, who'd spoken to him, was surprised by his abrupt manner and his insistence that he didn't want anything to remember his uncle by. He told her to auction anything that could bring in a few pounds and that he would pay them to get rid of everything else. Clearly, Tim and his Uncle Pete had not been close.

Dotty passed a single-storey, pebble-dashed village hall and, on the next bend, Kingham's stone church with a large graveyard, enclosed by a low stone wall.

Pete Reynolds's end-of-terrace, two-storey stone cottage was easy to find, situated opposite the village's large pub, The Wild Rabbit. There was just enough room to park her car in the narrow drive between the cottage and the imposing three-storey detached house next door.

Inside, the cottage was just as she had expected for an occupant who had been in his late nineties. The rear kitchen was small and poky, with brown units and a beige and cream linoleum floor that clearly hadn't been upgraded since the mid-1980s.

When she opened a wall cupboard, she noticed the neatly arranged tins and an assortment of sauces and condiments which looked as if they had been there for years, their labels slightly faded, but everything had its place.

She could bundle together the better-quality kitchen items, but even three or four boxes of them were unlikely to make more than £20 or £30 at auction.

It was obvious Pete had been thrifty. In the small sitting room, beneath brown and grey throws, she found a faded, garishly floral three-piece suite with holes in the arms. It wasn't worth selling.

Neither was much else in the room, although the desk under the stairs looked more promising. Approaching it, she realised it was a solid, late Victorian writing desk, and the brass cup handles appeared original. The green leather top was scuffed and damaged, but perhaps that only added to its charm.

As she moved back to take in the full view, her gaze was drawn to a small landscape painting hanging above the desk and, dangling from it, a pendant with a small figure on the end.

She stepped forward and unhooked the chain from around the picture to examine the pendant more closely. It was in the shape of an owl, with two mismatched coloured stones for eyes. Turning it over, she noticed the maker's mark of a crescent moon within a circle. Weighing the figure in her hand, she considered it could be gold, although there were no hallmarks to confirm this. And were the eyes coloured glass or gems?

It was an interesting decorative item and one worth considering further. And the painting it had hung from? Clearly it held some meaning for Pete, but she wasn't sure about its value. The style suggested the early twentieth century, with a traditional yet romanticised depiction of a rural scene, rendered in warm, natural tones.

It was pleasant, although not to her personal taste. She'd take it back with her, along with the owl pendant.

Opening the top right drawer of the desk, she found the expected collection of pens, pencils, and other such items. But in the left drawer there was a bundle of letters and correspondence.

She'd take those back to look through, along with the coloured cardboard files she found in the next drawer down. It was a task their new, keen young receptionist, Clara Barrett, could work on.

Dotty climbed the wooden stairs to the first floor and discovered a bookcase in the main bedroom.

It contained some *Commando* and *The Eagle* comics, which might be worth five or ten pounds each, or more if they were rare editions.

There were also several military-themed first edition books, each potentially worth several hundred pounds. Given Pete's age, he had likely fought in the Second World War, which explained his interest in such books and comics.

Collecting some boxes from her car, she packed up the books and comics, the painting, the pendant, and the paperwork. These she'd take back with her.

The kitchen items which she placed in the remaining boxes could be delivered to Akemans, along with the oak desk, a mahogany chest of drawers, and several other nice, but not particularly high quality, pieces of furniture. Everything else could be donated to a local charity they used on such occasions.

Her task complete, she closed the front door of Pete's cottage, marking the end of his story. Or so she thought …

CHAPTER THREE

DOTTY

It was after one in the afternoon by the time Dotty arrived back at Akemans, following her inspection of the contents of Pete Reynolds's cottage.

She carried the box of Pete's most valuable possessions and paperwork into the front office area of the auction house.

Clara Barrett was sitting at the antique reception desk, eating a sandwich. In some ways, she was similar to Marion, who was sitting at a second desk facing the dividing wall between the auction house and the antique centre, although Clara was a third of Marion's age.

Both were petite and favoured a classical rather than fashionable dress style. But while Clara had a soft, round, kindly face, Marion's was seasoned by years and experience.

Marion kept her dark hair in a neat bob, similar to Dotty's, whereas Clara had tied back her light brown, wavy hair, which, when loose, fell to her shoulders.

The distinctive aroma of carrot and coriander soup from Marion's direction caused Dotty's stomach to rumble.

Clara looked at Dotty with large, expressive hazel eyes and asked, "Anything of interest at the house you visited?"

Placing the box on the brown, nylon-carpeted floor, Dotty removed the owl pendant and replied, "Not a great deal, but perhaps you could work through the box and register its contents for our next auction, whenever that is. And there's some paperwork I'd like you to look through. It's not urgent, but we should be thorough. And now," said Dotty, glancing at the lunches on both desks, "I think I'll pop through to the cafe and see if Keya is around."

Dotty considered Keya, who ran the Waterwheel Café, to be her best friend. As she opened the interconnecting door between the auction house and the antique centre, she remembered how they'd first met, before Dotty had even formally started working at Akemans. She'd inadvertently become involved in a police investigation after finding a body hidden in a grandfather clock.

Smiling wryly to herself, she dodged a splattering of white plaster dust on the stone floor of the large, open antique centre.

She hadn't known then that the case would be the first of several she'd help to solve. And it had been the beginning of her friendship with the energetic and, back then, often clumsy Constable Keya Varma.

Keya had since been promoted to sergeant, but she'd wanted to do more than just be a police officer. Two years ago, she'd agreed with Gilly to open a cafe at the rear of the ground floor of the old flour mill, in space not utilised by the antique centre.

Dotty reflected that Zach, who'd become a close part of her life over the past year, would have thought it an efficient use of space and an excellent diversification of the antique business.

She opened the door into the bright cafe space, lit by domed brass pendant lights and large, floor-to-ceiling windows that looked out over a working waterwheel and, beyond it, the River Coln.

She was delighted and relieved that at least one area of Akemans was still buzzing.

Keya's younger sister, Zivah, the middle of three girls, greeted Dotty.

"Late lunch?" she asked. "Aunt Beanie is just finishing hers if you'd like to join her, or I'll try to find a table of your own if you'd prefer."

"Um," uttered Dotty hesitating, and then she felt the owl pendant still clasped in her hand. Aunt Beanie might know something about the little trinket.

Zivah, who'd maintained her trim figure despite having a baby son, led her to a table situated close to the hot drinks serving counter. From behind it, Norman Climpson waved.

Though well into his sixties, Norman's sandy-coloured hair was only just starting to show strands of grey, but the broken veins in his permanently tanned face betrayed a man who'd spent most of his life outdoors. His beard was getting a little unruly again, and no doubt Aunt Beanie, with whom he shared a house, would have something to say about it.

"Good afternoon, dear," Aunt Beanie said as Dotty joined her at a vintage, square wooden table. "And what have you been busy with this morning?"

Aunt Beanie was everyone's favourite eccentric aunt, although she was not actually related to Dotty. She had offered her a cottage to live in at Meadowbank Farm on the edge of Fairford, a small Cotswold town about ten minutes' drive from Akemans.

"I've just returned from surveying a house clearance in Kingham, which is why I'm late for lunch."

"Anything of interest?" asked Aunt Beanie, raising a china teacup with a red and pink rose design. She had long, silver-white hair which she held back off her face with a series of brightly coloured scarves. Today's was a golden yellow, tied as she always did, with a large bow on top of her head.

"Not really. It was the home of a single man, and it doesn't look as if he'd made any changes since the 1980s. But I found a few first edition military history books and some comics, which might raise a little. Also, a very nice Victorian oak writing desk, and this." She placed the owl pendant on the table as Zivah handed her a laminated menu.

As Dotty examined the menu, which she knew by heart, Aunt Beanie scooped up the pendant.

"That's pretty," said Zivah. "An owl."

"Yes, and I believe it's made from gold," Aunt Beanie said as she peered at the pendant.

Dotty sensed movement to her right, but when she turned her head, the four people seated closest to her were calmly studying their menus.

Aunt Beanie also glanced towards the adjacent table as Zivah said, "Today's specials are carrot and coriander soup, pea, mint and ricotta quiche, and baked potatoes with a creamy leek and cheddar cheese filling."

At the nearby table, an elderly man with wispy white hair and a hunched posture looked up at Zivah with alert, deep-set eyes in his narrow face. He gestured to her.

"Excuse me," said Zivah, moving toward him.

"That's Matthew Henshaw," whispered Aunt Beanie, leaning closer to Dotty. "He owns and runs Athena Trading, a successful import-export business. He's with his grandchildren, Imogen and Seb." Sitting on either side of the elderly man were an attractive, well-dressed pair in their late twenties or early thirties.

"And who's the man talking to Zivah?" asked Dotty, referring to a lean man with salt-and-pepper hair and an erect posture, who was pointing to something on the menu.

"That's Matthew's right-hand man, Radek Novák," replied Aunt Beanie as Radek turned and smiled appreciatively at Zivah.

"He's a charmer, that's for sure, but he's fiercely protective of Matthew and indispensable in both business and charity matters. Which is more than can be said for Seb. He enjoys entertaining clients at Cheltenham races, but I hear he's of little use in the business."

"And the granddaughter?" Dotty asked, sure she'd seen her or her image recently.

"Ah, now there's someone I respect. Taking the disappointment of being excluded from the family business purely because she's a woman, Imogen skipped university and started working at a small tech start-up as a marketing assistant. By the age of twenty-five, she'd launched her own business, BrightEdge Solutions."

"That's why I've heard of her. Zach showed me the company profile online recently. They specialise in digital marketing, and he thought we might utilise their skills."

"With the auction house?" Aunt Beanie asked sharply.

"Yes, and maybe we can persuade Gilly to consider a strategy for the antique centre. We have to do something to revive Akemans' reputation."

"Is it that bad?" asked Aunt Beanie. "I heard you were merging April's auction with Cirencester Auctioneers again."

"It's not just the damage the newspaper allegation did. We're outdated and stuck in our ways. But change and modernisation cost money, which, apparently, we don't have to invest in the business at the moment."

Aunt Beanie placed her hand on Dotty's and said reassuringly, "I'm sure we'll be able to weather the storm. And if you need any help with my brother, just ask."

"Thank you," Dotty replied gratefully. She might well need to call on Aunt Beanie's assistance if she was going to discuss business changes with Marmaduke Carey.

"And now, this little owl figure. Do you recognise the mark on the back? The crescent moon in the circle?"

"Should I?" Dotty asked. Were her antique skills failing her as well as her business ones?

"Not necessarily. It belongs to a post-war immigrant jeweller named Otto Mond. The circle is for Otto and the crescent moon is for Mond. He didn't make many pieces while he lived in England. A few in the internment camp where he was placed during the war, and more afterwards, but he died in 1951. This little pendant could fetch a fair sum, perhaps £5,000. More if you can discover who commissioned it and why. It is made from gold, despite not having the regulatory hallmarks, and I'd wager its eyes are precious stones. It wouldn't surprise me if it was made from a larger object Otto melted down."

"You mean stolen treasure?" Dotty asked, intrigued.

"Possibly, or more likely a weightier, recognisable piece smuggled over and reworked into manageable items to sell and raise funds. It was common before, during, and after the war with refugees from Germany and later those from the Iron Curtain states."

As Dotty took back the owl pendant, she again felt someone watching her. She turned to the adjacent table, where both Matthew Henshaw and his assistant, Radek, were staring at her.

Matthew inclined his head and smiled, but Radek's watchful gaze remained fixed on Dotty. Feeling uncomfortable, she turned back to Aunt

Beanie. Then she looked down at the small golden owl and murmured under her breath, "What secrets could you tell?"

CHAPTER FOUR

DOTTY

Dotty was enjoying her bowl of carrot and coriander soup with a ham and salad roll at the Waterwheel Cafe.

Aunt Beanie had finished her tea and left for gardening club, leaving Dotty alone. She tried her best not to listen to the conversation at the nearest table. But…

"Surely we don't all need to go tonight," Seb, the grandson, complained. "It's only a talk by some unknown author who's written a book on treasures lost during wars. It's of no interest to me at all."

"And you'd rather be taking a striking blonde out

for the evening in Cheltenham," Imogen, the granddaughter, said mischievously.

Dotty bit into her roll, wondering whether the talk they were discussing was part of the inaugural literary festival being run by a group of book enthusiasts in Stow-on-the-Wold. She knew Zach had bought tickets to support several of the events. In fact, one of them might even be that evening.

"Hiya," Keya said, settling into Aunt Beanie's vacated seat with a cup of tea. "You're late having lunch."

Dotty smiled at her friend, whose warm brown complexion, lively eyes, and ready grin always brightened her mood. Her dark hair was scraped back into a ponytail, and there was a white stain on her bright blue top.

Noticing Dotty's gaze, Keya looked down and exclaimed, "Oh, toda!" which was one of her favourite expressions. "Not again. That's the second top I've spilt mayonnaise on today. Mick and I are trying out a new recipe using wild garlic."

Mick was one of her chefs. He was a large man with several tattoos on his arms, which he'd acquired while in prison for a crime he hadn't committed. On his release, Keya had offered him a job in the cafe, and he was hard-working, loyal, and grateful. With little personal life, he loved nothing better than baking cakes and creating new dishes for the cafe.

"So what have you been doing?" Keya asked.

Dotty told her about her visit to Kingham. "And what about you? Has your crime scene at Lechlade been wrapped up?"

"Yes, it turned out to be a group of teenagers playing a prank for a birthday party," Keya replied, rolling her eyes.

Dotty regarded her friend, who had given up, or rather moved on from, her job as a sergeant at Cirencester police station to take on a new role as a crime scene manager. "You don't seem very excited about the new position."

"It's OK, it's just not…" Keya's voice trailed off.

"As exciting as investigating murders?" Dotty suggested.

"Yes, but does that sound awful?" Keya regarded Dotty, her eyes wide and bright.

"It's understandable, but I heard Sujin say you have to start small and prove yourself before you can move on to larger crime scenes."

"I know, and he's right, but it's still frustrating. Not that I could have continued investigating such cases at Cirencester anyway, after the murder squad at Headquarters took over serious crimes."

"How is Inspector Lynn managing? She's still investigating dead bodies when they turn up," Dotty said.

"It helped that she cleared up several old cases, and she doesn't complain when the murder squad hands over the ones they think are boring… or beneath them. Warren even overheard one of them say something like, 'What's the point in sending us out to investigate when it's just another village squabble gone wrong? If someone gets bumped off over a charity cake sale or a dispute about a garden fence, it's hardly worth our time.'"

Inspector Lynn Lockwood had joined Cirencester Police Station in January, and Constable Wayne

Sparrow was the only member of Keya's original team who had stayed.

"Anyway, that's enough about work," said Keya with finality. "Are you and Zach still coming to the Hotel Du Vin on Saturday night to watch the Celtic Twisters?"

The Celtic Twisters was the name of the ceilidh band that Keya's boyfriend, Sujin, played in. He'd also worked at Cirencester Police Station but had recently been promoted to Regional Forensic Operations Coordinator.

Dotty knew he was thrilled about the new role, although she wasn't entirely sure what it involved. However, she did enjoy listening to the band's live sessions, and she and Zach were looking forward to seeing them perform at the Cheltenham Music Festival.

"Shall I book us a table for supper before or after the session?" Keya asked.

"What time are they playing?" enquired Dotty.

"Seven, so they'll be finished by half past eight."

"Let's go for afterwards then, so Sujin will be able

to relax. As long as that's OK with you? I don't have to work on Sunday, but you do."

"I'll ask Zivah if she can open up the cafe," Keya replied. "Do you have any other plans for the weekend?"

"I think Zach has bought tickets for some of the readings and book launches at the Stow-on-the-Wold Literary Festival. I need to check if I'm supposed to go with him to one tonight."

"Sounds more your thing than mine," Keya said, glancing round the cafe. "I guess I better get back to work."

"Me too," replied Dotty, whose bowl and plate were now empty. "Can you add this to my tab? I suppose I ought to focus on this month's auction, even though we're not holding it here."

Keya gave her friend a lopsided smile and squeezed her shoulder as she stood up. "Don't worry. You'll figure it out."

But would she? Dotty wondered as she watched Keya stride off, narrowly avoiding bumping into a chair. And would her troubles with the auction house affect Keya's cafe?

CHAPTER FIVE

DOTTY

Dotty loved the lengthening spring days, and it was still light as she and Zach arrived in Stow-on-the-Wold for a talk about the search for lost wartime treasures.

During her work, Dotty had come across a few items whose provenance was either untraceable or unknown. She'd often wondered if they had originated from war torn areas.

But then, the British were still being criticised for the artefacts they had taken, some would say plundered, from countries they'd colonised hundreds of years ago.

"I think this will be interesting," Zach said as he parked his black Jeep beside the pavement on a quiet side street in the Cotswold town.

They had already driven past the venue, a local bookshop called The Owl's Nook, and seen its full car park.

"And if the number of cars we saw is anything to go by, it's certainly well supported," Zach added.

He smiled as he linked his arm through Dotty's, and they strolled unhurriedly back towards the bookshop.

"How did you find out about the talk?" Dotty asked, wondering if helping her at Akemans had sparked his interest in antiques and lost treasures.

"I've visited The Owl's Nook a few times," he said, his words slowing slightly, as though he were choosing them carefully.

"Oh, yes?" Dotty asked, intrigued.

"I know I said I didn't want to know anything more about my grandfather and great uncle, but, well, I changed my mind."

"Because Keya and I found the legacy they left in a London safe deposit box?"

Zach, with Dotty's help, had followed a trail of letters and valuable objects left by his great uncle Robert. But when he discovered that the siblings had been part of a notorious New York gang during the Depression, and that his grandfather Harry had been imprisoned for shooting another gang member, he had refused to delve any deeper into his family history.

She had also found evidence suggesting Zach's grandfather was innocent and had likely shouldered the blame for his brother Robert, who was later killed in France during World War II, while serving in a British regiment.

But now it seemed Zach's interest in his family heritage had been rekindled.

"The Owl's Nook has a section on military history, particularly the Second World War," Zach explained, "so I've started to read a bit about it."

"That's great," Dotty said enthusiastically as they looked both ways before crossing the road.

The Owl's Nook looked like a converted Victorian school or a similar period building. Its long honey-coloured stone façade faced the road, featuring three arched windows and two dormer ones set into the sloping grey slate roof.

To the right, there was a small stone entrance porch, and to the left, the gable end of another stone structure with a larger arched window. Outdoor tables and chairs were arranged in front of and to the side of this section.

"There's also a popular cafe," said Zach, noticing the direction of Dotty's gaze, and then he added, "But don't tell Keya that I visit it sometimes."

"Keya doesn't expect us to only go to her cafe, and it's a great idea combining one with a bookshop. Where will the talk be held?"

"I presume in the main bookshop area, which is the building facing us," Zach replied as they walked across the gravel parking area towards the stone entrance porch. Above the open doorway, a small owl was carved into the stone, alongside the Latin inscription *Per Aspera Ad Successum*.

"'Through hardship to success'," Zach translated.

"I asked about it before because I don't know any Latin."

Inside the porch, a wooden stand held leaflets about activities and events in the Cotswolds, with a map of the area hanging above it. They stepped into the main bookshop, where a till and serving counter were positioned near the entrance.

Beyond them, bookshelves lined the outer walls, while freestanding units filled the back of the room. The central area had been cleared, with rows of black metal chairs with blue seats, the kind often seen in office reception areas, neatly arranged facing a small platform set up behind the entrance door.

To the right, bookshelves stood packed closely together, and Dotty realised they were on wheels and had been moved to create the open space.

She followed Zach into the room where people were clustered in groups or already sitting on the rows of chairs.

Dotty glanced upwards as a lady with curly grey hair, wearing a long, embroidered, midnight blue tunic over wide-legged linen trousers, approached Zach and clasped his hand.

"Zach, thank you for supporting us," the woman greeted him in a strong yet warm voice.

Dotty took in the wooden banister of the gallery that ran around the room at a higher level, with shelves of books continuing up to the ceiling.

"And this must be Dotty. I've seen you at auctions, but we've never met," said the woman, smiling warmly at her.

"This is Helen, and this," said Zach, raising his arms, "is her bookshop, The Owl's Nook."

"Lovely to meet you," Dotty replied, "and I was just admiring your place. So many books, and what a wonderful idea to have portable bookshelves."

"That was my daughter, Laura's, idea when we refurbished the place. It means we can create a sizeable space for events like this.

"And you have a great turnout," Zach said approvingly as he looked around. More people were entering through the stone porch.

"Thankfully. Which will please this evening's sponsor," Helen said giving Zach a relieved look.

Several banners around the bookshop advertised the book launch and talk and at the bottom Dotty saw the sponsors name was Athena Trading. Beside it was a stylised bird which could be an eagle … or an owl she considered as Zach spoke.

"I see Matthew Henshaw is sponsoring tonight's event."

Dotty looked up at Zach and said, "He was at Keya's cafe a few days ago. What exactly does he do?"

"His company Athena Trading deals in all sorts of consumer goods, but round here people know him more for his charity work and for supporting local events like this," Zach said.

Helen adjusted her tunic, and the movement caused her necklace to slip into view.

Dotty gasped as the people around her started to murmur.

"Excuse me," said Helen as she moved easily around Dotty and Zach.

"What is it?" asked Zach, his voice full of concern.

"Helen's necklace. The owl pendant looks just like one I found during a house clearance this week, although the eyes are different."

"Is that such a surprise? There's probably a local shop which sells them."

Dotty turned to Zach, frowning slightly and said, "Aunt Beanie told me the one I have was made by a jeweller after the war. He only made a few pieces in England before he died so, yes, it is a surprise to see the same piece."

Zach smiled. "As you can tell, Helen has a bit of an obsession with owls, so I'm not surprised she has one as a necklace. And now that Matthew Henshaw and his party have arrived, it looks like they're preparing to start. We should find our seats."

CHAPTER SIX

DOTTY

Dr Hugo Marston ran his hand absently through his sandy brown hair and said, "Good evening everyone, and, goodness, thank you. I wasn't expecting such a turnout. I was told Stow-on-the-Wold was a sleepy little town, but that clearly isn't true."

He paused, scanning the audience.

If his comment was meant as a joke, it hadn't landed. Nervously, he pushed his wire-framed glasses up his nose. Adopting a more formal tone, he introduced himself, recounting his academic qualifications. A first in History and Archaeology from Oxford University and a PhD focusing on art provenance during World War II, particularly Nazi-looted treasures.

His career began at the British Museum, where he specialised in tracing the provenance of contested artefacts.

"And now, I am Director of Provenance and Restitution at the International Art Recovery Alliance," Dr Marston concluded with pride.

"Impressive bio," whispered Zach.

Dr Marston continued, "During World War II, the Nazis orchestrated the largest art theft in history, seizing over 650,000 artworks across Europe. While many pieces have been recovered and returned, a significant number remain unaccounted for. Estimates suggest between 30,000 and 100,000 works of art are still missing, with a combined value in the billions of pounds."

"Wow," Dotty murmured.

"That is why, some eighty years after the war ended, governments, organisations, and individuals continue to seek the restitution of these cultural artefacts and their return to their rightful owners or their descendants."

At the front of the audience, Dotty noted Matthew Henshaw's wispy grey-haired head nodding, while his assistant, Radek, sat bolt upright beside him. At the edge of the front row, Seb stretched his legs into the aisle, then crossed them, glancing back through the audience. Catching Dotty's eye, he smiled mischievously.

Dotty quickly returned her attention to the speaker. Dr Marston explained how his grandfather, a World War II veteran, inspired his career through stories about recovering looted treasures in Germany.

He shared anecdotes about returning a stolen Van Gogh painting to its rightful heirs and uncovering a hidden cache of Nazi-looted artefacts in an Austrian monastery.

Dotty glanced round the audience, observing that most attendees were in their sixties or older. Perhaps that wasn't surprising, given the topic. Few young people cared about the Second World War, having no memory of it or its aftermath.

Imogen Henshaw wasn't sitting with her family, but next to Helen, whose blue tunic top Dotty recognised. She wasn't sure who the other two women with them were.

"Helen's daughter, Laura, and her granddaughter, Beth," whispered Zach, who had an unsettling knack of reading Dotty's thoughts tonight.

Dr Marston concluded with the story of 'The Woman in Gold', an iconic painting by Gustav Klimt stolen from a Jewish family in Austria. Decades later, a surviving family member launched a legal battle to reclaim it. After years of struggle, the painting was finally returned in 2006.

"This painting," Dr Marston said, "is more than a work of art. It's a vessel of memory and resilience, a reminder that treasures like these carry the stories of those who fought to reclaim not just their heritage, but also their identities."

It was a compelling and passionate ending to the talk, which had been far more interesting than Dotty had expected.

"That wasn't as dry as I'd feared," Zach said as they and the rest of the audience clapped their appreciation.

Raised on the small stage, Dr Marston stood awkwardly, a faint flush creeping up his neck. He adjusted his glasses, gave a modest wave, and offered a shy, slightly crooked smile.

"Thank you, truly," he said self-consciously.

One of the women near Helen rose, still clapping, and walked to the stage. She climbed onto the platform, turned to the audience, and, with a poise reminiscent of a headmistress bringing her pupils to order, waited for the audience to settle.

She delivered a brief but polished thank you, concluding, "Dr Marston will now be signing copies of his book at the front of the stage. Beth, Nicole?"

Dotty watched as two younger women carried a table already laden with books. Both had slightly rounded figures, contrasting with the athletic Imogen Henshaw, who followed carrying a heavy-looking box.

Imogen said something to the younger girl, whose dark auburn hair was clipped back neatly on both sides. The older one, with tightly drawn features, gave the audience a steady, watchful look, her tight smile vanishing as Imogen turned towards her.

“Ah, Dotty, I’ve been meaning to speak with you,” said a middle-aged man as he approached her. “But with the newspaper allegations and Georgina’s departure…”

Dotty stood and reassured him that Akemans remained a reliable and professional business. She even offered to visit him to discuss selling some collectibles and vintage trinkets.

Sensing his hesitation, and suspecting he doubted her abilities, she added, “I could ask Marion Rook to accompany me.”

“Marion? How is she? I thought she’d left Akemans after…” His voice trailed off.

“She’s doing very well and is a great asset to the auction house. Shall we say ten o’clock on Tuesday?” suggested Dotty, eager to secure the appointment.

“Um, yes, why not? Ten o’clock next Tuesday,” agreed the man. Dotty took down his details and felt relieved as he walked away. Would every piece of business require such effort?

She looked around and spotted Zach standing in the queue to purchase a signed book. The pinched-faced girl, who she guessed worked in the bookshop, stood beside Dr Marston, taking payment for the books he'd signed.

At the back of the room, Dotty noticed a table set out with drinks and nibbles. She approached and helped herself to a glass of white wine as Helen's voice carried over the low hum of conversation.

She glanced up to see Helen standing with Matthew Henshaw and Radek Novák.

Leaning heavily on a wooden walking stick, Matthew said, "Dr Marston's words truly moved me. I personally saw some of the treasures he spoke of during the war. Looted artefacts and relics of incredible beauty and craftsmanship. But at the time..."

He paused for a moment, his gaze distant, before continuing, "They were just objects to me. In the face of what I witnessed, the atrocities and the sheer inhumanity, I didn't see their importance."

Helen nodded, her face soft with understanding. "I imagine it was hard to focus on anything beyond the devastation to people's lives."

Matthew nodded sincerely. "The things I witnessed." He paused, seeming to compose himself, "But that is not tonight's topic. Hearing how Dr Marston described those treasures as vessels of memory, resilience, and identity, made me realise I've been wrong to dismiss their significance. These aren't just things. They're links to the past. To people who were robbed of so much more than their possessions."

Radek shifted uneasily, his jaw tightening almost imperceptibly, but Matthew didn't appear to notice.

Dotty sipped her wine, peering over the rim of her raised glass at Matthew as he said, "Perhaps it's time I did more." His voice was quiet but resolute. "Set some things right. Support the organisations working to recover what's been lost. And maybe, in some small way, help those who still suffer because of war, religion, or where they were born."

Helen reached out and gently touched his arm. "That's an admirable thought, Matthew. It's never too late to do some good. And thank you for sponsoring tonight's event. It was personal to me and my family too. Like Dr Marston, I grew up listening to my father's wartime tales, especially about a hoard of stolen Nazi treasure his unit discovered at the end of the war, and a young interpreter who saved them when he spotted an ambush."

Matthew shifted his cane and leaned closer to Helen. "And where was this?" he asked.

"A part of Germany called Saxony," she replied. "It became part of East Germany, and my father's unit had to withdraw as a Russian one moved in. But, worried about the treasure, they loaded as much as they could into the US army trucks they'd acquired and returned to England. I feel proud now, listening to Dr Marston's speech, that he handed the treasure over. Except…"

"Except?" queried Matthew, his full attention on Helen.

"We recently found a wooden box in a trunk of his wartime possessions I'd forgotten about. Its origin is clearly Jewish, and I'm concerned it's part of the Nazis' stolen treasure."

"And the owl pendant you're wearing around your neck?" Radek asked, his eyebrows rising.

"Oh no, this isn't from the war," Helen said quickly. "At least I don't think it is. I only recently rediscovered it amongst my father's possessions. I know it was precious to him, and he always kept it with him, so it's no wonder I have a penchant for owls."

"And so do I," said Matthew, "and a very attractive little owl it is too, don't you think, Radek?"

For a brief moment, Dotty caught a wary look in Radek's eyes, but then he smiled and agreed, "Very nice. But now, sir, I think I should take you home."

CHAPTER SEVEN

DOTTY

Dotty walked arm in arm with Zach through Cheltenham's fashionable Montpellier district, where the town's Regency architecture was on full display.

The Hotel du Vin occupied one of the classical Georgian buildings, and its elegant symmetry, tall sash windows, and stone portico entrance were characteristic of the period.

Inside the hotel's spacious lobby, they were greeted by a striking spiral staircase and a polite member of staff whose name badge told Dotty he was called Ben.

"Good evening, madam, sir. Are you here for the music, or will you be staying with us?" Ben asked with a welcoming smile.

Dotty was captivated by the relaxed atmosphere and timeless elegance of the hotel and thought that she would like to stay one day.

"We're here for the music," Zach replied.

"Tonight's performance will be held in our bistro. Drinks will be served throughout, and food will be available before and after the performance," the man said in a courteous tone.

"I think my friend has already booked a table. Keya Varma," Dotty said, her voice anxious as she wondered if Keya had remembered to make the reservation.

"Of course. Miss Varma is already here, seated in one of our perimeter booths." The man led them through the lobby and into a chic room furnished with dark brown leather chairs and upholstered seating along the walls.

Polished wooden floors gleamed under the warm cream walls, and the space was still illuminated by natural light filtering through tall windows.

At the far end, Sujin and his bandmates were setting up their equipment. Their instruments were simple. An accordion for the band's leader, Figgy MacGillivray, together with a guitar, a flute and Sujin's violin, or fiddle, as he preferred to call it.

The room hummed with chatter as the audience gathered. Dotty quickly spotted Keya who was standing to one side, waving energetically.

Ben melted away as Dotty and Zach navigated round the tables and clusters of standing guests towards Keya.

"Hiya!" Keya greeted them cheerfully. "This is a bit swankier than the band's usual gigs."

Dotty and Zach settled on the tall, padded bench with Keya, chatting idly while the room steadily filled up.

Among the gathering crowd, Dotty spotted several familiar faces and prominent figures from the Cotswolds, including the stooped figure of Matthew Henshaw. But tonight, he was accompanied by an elderly, well-dressed couple and escorted to a table in the middle of the room.

When Zach suggested ordering a bottle of champagne, the sommelier instead recommended a Viognier Les Iles Blanches. Both Dotty and Zach were impressed by its bold, fruity flavours. Keya, who didn't drink alcohol, ordered a virgin passionfruit mojito, although Dotty wasn't sure about the floating seeds as Keya sucked on her straw.

Just after seven, the curtains were drawn against the evening dusk and Figgy stood up and introduced himself and the band.

They played a mixture of instrumental reels and lyrical ballads, gradually increasing the tempo and energy as the evening progressed and the audience, who were probably more used to classical performances, warmed to them.

"And now, for our final song. You may know it, so please join in as we all sing Molly Malone," encouraged Figgy.

Dotty tapped her feet while Zach, who had a surprisingly good voice, joined in on the chorus. As the clapping and cheers subsided, Dotty noticed Keya reaching for her phone. She covered one ear, straining to hear the caller over the noise, and her face tightened.

A flushed and bright-eyed Sujin was weaving through the tables toward them when he also paused to check his phone. He read something on the screen before locking eyes with Keya. A silent understanding passed between them.

Keya turned to Dotty and Zach and said in an apologetic tone, "I'm really sorry, but I, we, have to go. A body's been discovered, and I've been asked to manage the scene." Despite the unfortunate news, her eyes gleamed with excitement. "My first murder case," she blurted.

"How do you know it's murder?" asked Dotty.

"Because the victim has a large gash on the side of her head," Sujin responded as he joined them.

"It could be an accident," Dotty suggested, hopefully. "She might have fallen."

Keya shook her head and said, "Warren is the first responder, and he thinks it's murder."

Dotty wondered if Warren's suspicion stemmed from having been part of Keya's team at Cirencester Police Station, where even accidental deaths seemed to take a sinister twist when Keya and, dare she say, herself were involved.

“Anyway, we have to go,” said Keya regretfully, glancing at a waiter carrying a bowl of risotto and a plate of beef steak with chunky chips. “And miss supper.”

Dotty watched them leave as Zach said, “Looks like it’s just the two of us. What do you fancy?”

CHAPTER EIGHT

KEYA

Keya sat quietly beside Sujin as he urged his RAV4 to pick up speed along the A40 heading east out of Cheltenham.

Her crime scene bag rested on the back seat, surrounded by the peculiar assortment of items Sujin kept in his car 'just in case'. Among them were a pink-handled child's fishing net, a lone golf club, and a telescopic fruit picker for retrieving objects caught in trees.

"Is there a reason we've both been called to this crime scene?" Keya asked, breaking the silence.

"Well, you need to secure and manage access to the scene, while I need to assess what forensic support the police will require. Between us, we'll decide which items, if any, to prioritise for analysis."

"The murder weapon, I presume, if we can find it," Keya said thoughtfully.

"I know Warren called it a murder, but we must stay professional and keep an open mind. This might be an accident, a suicide, or something else. It's not necessarily foul play."

"I know," Keya replied, though she couldn't help the flicker of anticipation in her voice. "So, what do we know?"

"The victim is seventy-two-year-old Helen Fletcher," Sujin began.

"And she didn't die of natural causes?"

"That will be for the pathologist to confirm. The police will also need to check her medical records."

"I wonder who'll be assigned to the case," Keya mused. "I hope it's Inspector Lynn."

"It depends on whether the murder squad considers it high-profile enough. But since our victim died in her own bookshop, I expect they'll dismiss it as another 'quirky' Cotswold case."

"Oh, let's hope so," Keya said, her voice tinged with eagerness.

As they turned onto the A429, also known as the Fosse Way, the linear Roman road stretched ahead, guiding them north-east towards Stow-on-the-Wold.

Sujin slowed as they approached the crime scene. An old stone building, flanked by a gravel car park which was now crowded with two police cars, an ambulance, and several unmarked vehicles.

"Here we go. Good luck," said Sujin, flashing Keya an encouraging smile as he turned off the engine. "Take your time. The victim is already dead, so the best thing we can do for her is to be thorough. Don't let anyone rush you."

Keya's mouth felt dry, and the weight of her responsibilities hit her. Any mistake she made could jeopardise the whole case and potentially allow a killer to go free.

But she couldn't afford to dwell on that. She just needed to remember that over her sixteen-year career, she had attended and processed countless crime scenes.

Climbing out of the car, Keya grabbed her crime scene bag and followed Sujin across the car park. As they approached the stone entrance porch, she noticed the owl carved above the door and the Latin inscription beneath it.

A constable she didn't recognise stood at the entrance, speaking firmly with a portly woman who claimed to be a friend of the deceased and was insistent on seeing her. Keya nodded in acknowledgment as she passed and entered the single-storey stone building.

The interior was much as she'd expected. A quaint bookshop with rows of neatly arranged shelves. The end panels bore labels describing the books on the shelves, while more books lined the walls and the upper gallery which ran around the edge of the building.

"Hi, Keya," Constable Warren Sparrow greeted her. "I'm glad you're managing this scene. I hope I've done everything right."

"I saw the constable at the door. Good job. How many people have entered the scene?"

"Just the bookshop assistant, Nicole Blake, who found the body. And the deceased's daughter and granddaughter, who Nicole called. Then there's me, Inspector Lynn, and a paramedic who confirmed the death."

"Not bad," Keya noted, glancing around. "And everyone's wearing protective footwear."

Sujin had moved to an area behind the shop's counter and was pulling on a paper forensic suit. Keya realised she'd better do the same.

A few minutes later, suited, booted, with her hood pulled up, and wearing two pairs of latex gloves, Keya emerged from behind the counter.

Remember, she told herself, it wasn't her job to piece together the clues and find the culprit. Her focus was on preserving and collecting evidence. First, she needed to determine whether the bookshop was the primary crime scene.

She moved across to a set of bookshelves in the far-right corner of the building, where Sujin was speaking quietly to Inspector Lynn Lockwood.

Lynn was wearing jeans and a padded jacket, her straight brown hair tied back practically in a ponytail.

She was of average height and had the build of a typical mum, not athletic but lean from constantly being on the go and balancing her work as a police officer with her role as a single mother to her eight-year-old daughter, Emily.

Finally, Keya saw the body sprawled on the wooden floor beside a bookshelf labelled *Historical Mysteries*. Her curly grey hair was dyed red, not by choice but by blood, and the pool on the floor confirmed this was the primary crime scene.

"My priority is to find the object she was struck with or struck her head against," Lynn said.

"I agree," Sujin replied. "But you'll need to discuss the search procedure with Keya."

Taking a deep breath, Keya stepped forward. "My immediate focus is to preserve any vulnerable evidence, particularly around the body. Has a pathologist been called to examine it in situ, or have you requested a Scene of Crime Officer?"

"Um," Lynn hesitated, glancing at Sujin.

"We thought, since you and I are here, we could handle those roles," Sujin said. "The body has been here for at least three hours…"

"So we don't want to waste any more time," Keya finished practically.

Lynn looked relieved.

Keya and Sujin worked efficiently. She photographed the scene and collected evidence around the body, while Sujin carefully examined the body itself. Nearly an hour later, Keya straightened up, stretching her back.

Sujin had finished his assessment, so she beckoned to the paramedic who was leaning against the entrance door frame. He disappeared briefly but returned with his colleague and a metal stretcher on wheels.

Keya stopped them several metres from the body, mindful of preventing contamination from the stretcher wheels, and instructed both paramedics to put on forensic booties before proceeding.

While the paramedics worked, Keya continued her photography, moving outwards from the body.

She reached shelves labelled ‘Geography’ and ‘Wildlife’.

And there was another owl. A wooden rather than stone one, sitting on a stand and staring at her with wide open eyes. Eyes that appeared to be crying. That wasn’t right. Owls weren’t carved with tears, were they?

She stepped closer and picked up the heavy wooden carving with her blue latex-gloved hand. She stared down at it, her pulse quickening as she realised the marks weren’t tears but splashes of blood.

She tightened her grip on the wooden owl and called out, her voice rising with excitement, “I’ve found the murder weapon!”

CHAPTER NINE

KEYA

Keya stood with Lynn outside the crime scene which she had been told was called The Owl's Nook bookshop.

They watched as Helen Fletcher's body was loaded into the back of the ambulance. Its destination was the new state-of-the-art mortuary in Gloucester, where the coroner would instruct a post-mortem examination to be undertaken.

Keya was grateful for the fresh air and took a deep breath, filling her lungs. Although it was night, the streetlights, the dim glow from the upstairs windows of nearby houses, and the clear moonlit sky created a muted twilight.

“Well, that’s done. Now I should start interviewing my suspects,” Lynn said with a sigh. Like Keya, her Saturday night plans had been ruined by the call-out.

“Who found the body?” Keya asked. Warren had already provided some initial details, but she wanted to hear what Lynn would add.

“The bookshop’s assistant, Nicole Blake. She’d been out delivering orders and was surprised to find the shop still open, even though Helen sometimes stayed late if a customer was searching for a specific book. But this time…” Lynn trailed off. “Nicole found her lying where you saw her.”

“No customers then?” Keya clarified.

“No, just Helen,” Lynn confirmed. “Nicole went straight to the house at the back of the shop and told Helen’s daughter, Laura, that her mother had fallen and was bleeding. Laura told Beth to call an ambulance while she returned to the shop with Nicole. Beth is Laura’s sixteen-year-old daughter.”

“Do they all live in the house behind the bookshop?” Keya asked.

"Yes. I don't know the full family dynamics yet, but no one's mentioned any husbands or a father."

Keya nodded. "I'd better get back inside, talk things through with Sujin, and decide how best to proceed."

Lynn smiled faintly. "And we're pretty sure the owl was the weapon which killed her?"

"I can't make any assumptions in my role as a crime scene manager," Keya said diplomatically. "But if I were still a sergeant at Cirencester, I'd say it's a strong working hypothesis."

"When did you start using such posh words?" teased Lynn.

"Must've been on my course or from living with Sujin. Do they suit me?" Keya stood a little taller, trying to look intellectual.

"Just don't start talking in theories instead of practicalities," Lynn said, shaking her head. "I need facts. But the advantage of having you here is that you can read the scene with a police officer's eye. Let me know your thoughts, even if they're off the record."

Keya considered Lynn's words as she returned to the bookshop, replacing her outer forensic booties with a fresh pair. Perhaps Lynn was right, and she could contribute more than just her technical expertise. She could also draw on her years of investigative experience.

"Keya, how would you like to proceed with processing the scene?" Sujin asked as he approached.

"Now the body has been removed, I'd like to do a thorough walk-through of the scene before more people disturb it. My initial theory is that Helen died where she was found."

"I agree, but let's not assume anything. We should start from the door and work through the bookshop. Don't forget the gallery level or the cafe next door. Customers were there until after five. And there's the house at the back."

Keya felt a flicker of panic and overwhelm at the job ahead. She took a steadying breath. "Let's focus on the bookshop first."

Sujin nodded. "That's sensible."

They began at the entrance, working their way methodically past the counter and into the main shop. Keya took in more details as they moved. The neatly arranged free-standing shelves, the perimeter displays, and the gallery above.

At the back of the shop, near a fireplace, there were two stylish armchairs. They weren't the sort you'd curl up in but more formal, matching the shop's character. There was plenty of dust and some rubbish in the area, but it showed no signs of a struggle, so Keya and Sujin moved on.

"Public locations are always more difficult to process," Sujin remarked. "Because of the amount of traffic and…" He ran a hand along a bookshelf displaying titles like *Being and Nothingness*, *Critique of Pure Reason*, and *The World as Will*, then held it up, revealing a thin layer of dust.

Looking up, Keya realised they were in a small section of books dedicated to philosophy.

She was grateful for Sujin's calm presence as they worked through the scene.

About two hours later, Warren appeared at the front door and called, "The inspector wants to know if you'd like a cuppa."

"Oh, yes, please," said Keya, relieved. She stood up and walked towards him, rolling her head from side to side to ease a crick in her neck. "How are you both getting on?"

Warren hesitated. "The granddaughter won't stop crying. She seems to think it's her fault somehow, although we don't know why. Her mum's in shock. And denial. Can't blame her. I mean, who'd want to bash in the head of an elderly bookshop owner?"

"Warren," Keya warned.

"Sorry," he muttered. "I just needed to let it out. I knew you'd understand."

"I do," Keya said, "but even if the victim seems like a typical Cotswold resident, what does that really mean? Did she have a secret life? Or something from her past she wanted to keep hidden? As Lynn asks the questions, listen carefully to the answers. And remember, it's not just what someone says, it's also what they don't."

"Thanks, Sarge," Warren said, then hesitated. "I mean… What should I call you now?"

"Keya's fine," she replied with a small smile. "Now go and fetch my tea. And a coffee for Sujin to keep him going."

CHAPTER TEN

DOTTY

"You look exhausted," Aunt Beanie said as Keya and Sujin sat down at the rectangular pine table in the large kitchen at Meadowbank Farm.

It was Sunday afternoon and rain was drumming against the tall windows at the conservatory end of the room.

Dotty looked over from the light-blue Aga, where she was stirring milk into a béchamel sauce on the cooler of the two large round hotplates.

"We were up most of the night processing a crime scene in Stow-on-the-Wold," Keya replied, "and grabbing a few hours' sleep during the day isn't the same as a full night's rest."

"What crime scene? Not a death, I hope," Aunt Beanie said, as Dotty turned back to her small black saucepan. She added another glug of milk and stirred the creamy mixture.

"I'm afraid so. An elderly bookshop owner."

Dotty froze. "What bookshop?" she asked, her voice tight, as she turned back towards the table.

"It's probably public knowledge by now, so I don't think there's any harm in telling you," Keya said, glancing at Sujin, who nodded his consent. "The Owl's Nook. The victim was a woman called Helen Fletcher."

"No!" cried Dotty.

"Did you know her?" Aunt Beanie asked sharply.

"Yes. Well, not really. Zach and I went to a talk at her bookshop on Thursday evening as part of the town's literary festival, and she was there. But you said victim. Does that mean it wasn't a natural death?"

Keya exchanged another glance with Sujin before answering, "There are some irregularities."

"What does that mean?" Dotty's voice rose, and she saw Keya press her lips together and lean back. "Come on, you can tell us," she urged.

"OK," Keya relented. "There was blood on her head and around the body. We think someone struck her with a wooden owl." She paused and added quickly, "But that's all conjecture." This time she didn't look at Sujin.

"What's that burning smell?" asked Aunt Beanie sniffing the air.

"Oh no!" cried Dotty. "My sauce!" Even her cat, Earl Grey, looked disgusted by her lack of concentration and culinary skills, as he stalked out of the kitchen with his tail held erect.

She moved the scorched pan to a marble slab and started again. As she melted butter and flour in a clean saucepan, Aunt Beanie asked, "So, what's your role in the investigation, Keya?"

"I'm managing the scene, securing it, and organising the collection of evidence. Usually, a team is assigned, but the murder squad doesn't see this as a high-priority case, so they've left it to Inspector Lynn to investigate and me to handle the crime scene work."

"Sujin helped me last night," she added, looking gratefully at him. "But I'll be on my own tomorrow."

"Perhaps you can rope Warren in to help, if Lynn doesn't need him," Sujin suggested.

Dotty stirred the butter and flour, her attention divided between her béchamel sauce and the conversation.

"Great idea," Keya said. "Then I can also quiz him about the suspects and Lynn's interviews."

"Keya," said Sujin, in a warning tone. "Your job is managing evidence at the scene, not speculating about suspects."

"I can't help wondering who did it," Keya said with a grin. "Old habits from working with Inspector Evans. Besides, Lynn asked for my input as an investigator, so I'm just following orders. Sort of," she added, looking smug.

Sujin sighed and gave her an exasperated look.

Dotty pulled the pan off the hotplate to stop the sauce burning, then turned and asked, “So, what’s next? Have you finished processing the scene?”

“We’ve worked on the area where the body was found,” Keya said. “I’ll double-check that, then move on to the cafe, the storage rooms, and probably the house. Just to be thorough.”

“And it gives you an excuse to nosy into the lives, habits, and possessions of potential suspects,” stated Aunt Beanie.

“The thought hadn’t crossed my mind,” Keya said with mock innocence.

“So, you’re going to be busy for the next few days,” Dotty said, turning back to her saucepan.

“Yes, but since it’s in the Cotswolds, I can still open up and organise the cafe before Zivah arrives from dropping young Kaami off at nursery,” Keya replied.

“Has your mum accepted that her grandson spends so much time at nursery and that Zivah is practically working full time for you?” Aunt Beanie asked.

"Zivah reached a compromise. Amma, our mum, will look after Kaami on Tuesday afternoons and all day Friday. At least, that's what she's doing at the moment, but we'll have to see if the arrangement lasts."

"I don't see why it won't. Your mother brought up three daughters of her own," Aunt Beanie remarked.

"True," Keya agreed. "And how are your parents?" she asked, raising her voice slightly.

Lifting the pan, Dotty turned to confirm the question was directed at her. Keya's concerned expression left no doubt it was.

"They're back in Edinburgh, and Dad has finally agreed to have some treatment. But there's little they can do except try to stop the cancer from spreading too quickly and ease his pain. Mum is back at work, which she feels conflicted about, but Dad says she needs something to do rather than fussing around him all day. And it's giving them both a break."

"And Zach?" Keya asked. "Does he like living in Burford?"

"Yes, I think so. He finds the shops convenient, but his area is quiet and away from the tourists."

"And...?" pressed Keya.

"And nothing," replied Dotty defensively.

"Where is he anyway?" asked Aunt Beanie. "You did tell him it was an early supper."

Dotty glanced at her watch. "I said supper at six, so he has time yet."

When Dotty's second béchamel sauce was finished successfully, she poured it over the leeks she had already cooked and sprinkled grated cheese over the top of the dish. Next, she checked the leg of lamb.

When she opened the top oven of the Aga, she was hit by the smell of garlic and rosemary. She had cut slits into the lamb and tucked in slivers of garlic and sprigs of the fragrant herb.

The roast spring vegetables and potatoes were also cooking well. Next, she prepared the Yorkshire pudding mixture, which was similar to a pancake batter.

She had just placed a muffin tin in the oven to heat the oil before adding the batter when Zach walked through the door carrying a bottle of red wine and a bunch of tulips and freesias.

"We were wondering where you were," Aunt Beanie said, standing and air-kissing Zach on each cheek. "And thank you," she added, taking the flowers and wine.

"Norman's just coming," said Zach.

"You've seen him?" asked Aunt Beanie in surprise.

"Yes, he called me to sort out an incident at the antique centre."

"Surely that's Gilly's responsibility," Aunt Beanie remarked.

"It is," said Zach, running a hand through his dark hair. "But Norman thought I'd handle it better, especially since he knows my concerns about the mill building and the structural survey you agreed I could commission."

"Oh dear. What happened?" asked Aunt Beanie, sounding worried.

“Nothing too serious this time,” Zach replied in a relieved tone. “A section of plaster fell from the ceiling near the wall with the auction house. It made quite a mess of the stall it landed on, and the owner declared he wouldn’t pay any more rent until the issue is sorted or his stall is moved.”

“You must speak to Gilly again. Or shall I?” asked Aunt Beanie. “We can’t let things like this keep happening. Not when Dotty and you are working so hard to rebuild Akemans’ reputation.”

“And there’s my cafe,” added Keya.

“Quite. Something has to be done,” declared Aunt Beanie. “What if someone is injured? Can you imagine what the press would make of that?”

CHAPTER ELEVEN

DOTTY

Dotty started work early at the auction house on Monday morning.

With squally rain showers and grey skies outside, she was grateful to be indoors, warming her hands around a cup of English Breakfast tea.

Her first task was to check on the progress of the catalogue for the end-of-month auction at Cirencester Auctioneers. It had to be sent to the printers by Wednesday to ensure delivery to local shops, post offices, and cafes by the weekend.

This month's edition was a straightforward black and white catalogue, with a single feature photograph of a sale item on each page. But they still needed to decide on eye-catching colour photographs for the front and back covers.

Perhaps the Audrey Johnson painting of spring flowers in a porcelain mug could go on the back. It was a pleasant, if not particularly valuable, piece.

Dotty flipped through the pages, making notes of those items that needed their descriptions updated, more photographs added, or an estimated price included.

For select pieces, particularly furniture, they needed condition reports that provided detailed descriptions of the item's state and noted any damage, wear or repairs. While all items were sold as seen, some bidders relied on these reports if they couldn't inspect the pieces in person beforehand.

She was debating whether to extend the description of a particularly elegant Edward VII three-piece silver tea service by Walker and Hall of Sheffield when the front door opened, and Marion stepped in, shaking her umbrella with dramatic flair.

"It's wild out there. My brolly nearly ended up in the next county," she declared.

Clara followed, pulling off a damp, grey wool beanie hat and tying her wavy hair back into a ponytail. She approached the front reception desk where Dotty was working.

"I was hoping to talk to you about the items you brought back from Pete Reynolds' house. I was going through the box on Friday," Clara said.

Dotty rolled her shoulders and leaned back. "Now's as good a time as any. I could use a break from working through the catalogue."

"I'll put the kettle on," Marion said as she headed to the small kitchenette at the back of the office.

Clara shrugged off her raincoat, hung it on the stand, and knelt beside the box of items from Pete Reynolds' estate. Dotty expected her to pull out the owl pendant, which she had put back in after her discussion with Aunt Beanie, or one of the books, so she was surprised when Clara removed the landscape painting instead.

"I wasn't sure that was worth much," Dotty admitted. "Have you found out otherwise?"

"She been very busy with her research," called Marion proudly as the kettle clicked off.

"At uni, we studied the revival in interest in Secessionist-era paintings that took place during the 1980s and 1990s," Clara began, carrying the painting across the room.

"And that means what, exactly?" Marion asked loudly as she poured boiling water into three mugs.

"Secessionist-era paintings came from the late nineteenth and early twentieth centuries in Europe, particularly Austria and Germany," Clara explained. "They were part of the Art Nouveau movement and are characterised by decorative, flowing lines, bold experimentation, and symbolic or modernist themes."

Dotty studied the painting as Clara placed it on the desk. "But this one looks traditional to me, romantic, even. It has flowing lines, sure, but no obvious modernist themes."

"Yes, the landscape subject is traditional," Clara agreed.

"And the composition is balanced and harmonious," Marion added, peering at the painting over Dotty's shoulder.

"But the bold colours and stylised forms reflect the influence of the Vienna Secession," Clara said. "The movement was all about breaking away from academic traditions."

"Now you sound like a website," Marion teased.

"Because she's researched the artist," Dotty guessed.

Clara nodded, picking up a notebook from the corner of the reception desk. "Josef Stoitzner, an Austrian artist, 1884 to 1951," she read. "He studied at the Academy of Fine Arts in Vienna."

"And?" Dotty prompted.

"His paintings currently sell for between £20,000 and £30,000," Clara finished, smiling triumphantly.

Marion whistled. "Not bad."

"Good work, Clara," Dotty said. "I'd never have guessed it was worth that much. I wonder how Pete got hold of it."

"That's where it gets interesting," Clara said. "While I couldn't trace this exact painting, it matches the descriptions of one of a set of three landscapes that went missing from a manor house in East Germany. One of them may have been sold at auction in Yorkshire last year."

"You're kidding," Dotty said, impressed.

"I found details of the seller and I'm planning to contact them today," Clara explained.

"That's excellent," Marion agreed.

"Well done, Clara," Dotty added. "What about the rest of the box?"

"The comics aren't particularly rare or valuable, but a collector might be interested," Clara said.

"And the books?" Dotty asked.

"I was going to start on those this morning, unless there's something else you'd like me to do?"

"We need to finish the auction catalogue," Dotty said. "Let me continue working through it but I might need your help with condition reports later."

The three of them settled into their tasks, working quietly for the next couple of hours. The only sounds were the occasional hiss of the kettle, the scratch of pens against paper, and the rhythmic click of keyboard keys. Dotty had nearly finished reviewing the catalogue when Clara's phone pinged, and she gasped.

"Oh no!" Clara exclaimed.

"What is it?" Dotty and Marion asked in unison.

"I've got alerts set for Akemans on social media. A new post is going viral. There's a person covered in plaster and dust at the antique centre, and another was narrowly missed by a falling basket!"

"Today or yesterday?" Dotty asked sharply.

"Today. Ten minutes ago," Clara replied.

Dotty picked up her phone, but it rang before she could dial.

"Hi, Zach," she answered.

"Where are you?" Zach asked.

"In the office. I've just heard about the antique centre."

"I'm on my way," Zach said.

Dotty heard the beep of his car unlocking, followed by the soft click of the door opening.

"Do you want me to do anything?" she asked.

"It depends how involved you want to be. It'd certainly help if you could go round and see what's happening, but the situation might be a bit volatile," Zach replied.

"I'll see if Marion will come with me."

At the sound of her name, Marion turned around in her chair and raised an eyebrow.

Finishing the call, Dotty looked at her. "We might be needed next door to help calm the situation. Are you up to it?"

"Of course," replied Marion, her tone serious.

They entered the antique centre through the interconnecting door. The vast, open-plan space had a high ceiling and rows of booths and stalls. In front of them, a metal staircase led up to the first floor, where Gilly's office was located.

Dotty turned towards the commotion on her right

and spotted Gilly running a hand through her mass of orange ringlets.

“I’m sorry for the mess the plaster caused, but this is an old building,” Gilly was saying, her tone strained. “We will, of course, compensate you for dry cleaning…”

She didn’t get the chance to finish. A smartly dressed woman covered in white plaster dust exclaimed, “Look at me! How can I go anywhere like this? And what if the basket had hit my friend? This place is a death trap!”

Hearing the exchange, Dotty and Marion hurried over. Before Gilly could respond, Dotty stepped in and said smoothly, “I’m very sorry for the distress this incident has caused. Why don’t we move next door, where it’s a bit quieter?”

“You just want to cover this up! Well, I’m not going anywhere,” the woman snapped.

“Do you really want pictures and videos of you covered in white plaster dust, with it in your hair and smeared across your face, spreading all over social media?” Marion asked practically.

"Well... no," the woman admitted, sounding uncertain.

"Then, please come with us, and we'll see what we can do," Marion said, her tone firm but calm.

"Come on, Bridget," her friend urged, tugging at her arm. "There's no point hanging around here."

Marion escorted the two women back to the auction house office while Dotty remained with Gilly.

"What are we going to do?" Gilly moaned, her wide eyes magnified by her large, orange-framed glasses. "First the mess on the stall yesterday, and now this? But Dad says we just don't have the money for repairs."

Dotty's brow furrowed, but she kept her voice steady as she said, "I think we'll have to find the money, but let's not dwell on that just yet. Zach's on his way, and we can talk it through with him. For now, let's focus on clearing up the mess. At least it didn't land on a stall this time."

Gilly took a deep breath, steadying herself, and nodded. "Of course, you're right. I'll fetch the hoover." She paused, then added, "You'd better go with Marion. I'm not sure what those women will demand… probably compensation, which we also can't afford."

"They weren't injured," Dotty pointed out. "It's their pride that's taken a hit. I'm not sure if they can sue us for that, or for the incident being captured and posted on social media. But…" She trailed off, looking thoughtful.

"But what?" Gilly asked, her tone worried.

"It's the damage incidents like this are doing to our reputation," Dotty muttered. "The stallholders are already upset, and if things like this put off customers …"

"Then we're in real trouble," Gilly groaned, finishing the thought. "I'll come through to the auction office and meet Zach after I've tidied up."

Dotty nodded, giving her a weak but reassuring smile before heading off to join Marion.

CHAPTER TWELVE

DOTTY

Dotty left Gilly to tidy up the mess caused by the falling plaster in the antique centre and returned to the auction house office.

She was relieved to find that the two women had gone, albeit with £100 each from petty cash to cover their cleaning costs and the distress the occurrence had caused them.

"Thank you so much," Dotty said, standing with Marion at the open front door, watching as the women climbed into a large white SUV.

"They really only wanted attention and a bit of money," responded Marion, shutting the door against the start of another April shower. "£100 each is cheaper than a legal wrangle or more posts going viral on social media."

Turning back to the office, Dotty saw Clara sitting at the front reception desk, the office phone to her ear. She heard her say, "Good morning, please can I speak to Mr Guy Watkins?"

After a pause, Clara added, "Clara Barrett, from Akemans auction house and antique centre."

Marion signalled a T shape with her fingers, suggesting a tea break, and Dotty nodded.

Clara continued, "Good morning, Mr Watkins. I'm calling from Akemans auction house in the Cotswolds, as I'm trying to authenticate a painting submitted for our next auction. It is a small landscape by Josef Stoitzner. We …"

Clara stopped mid-sentence, presumably listening to Mr Watkins speak.

The adjoining door to the antique centre opened, and Gilly bustled in, wiping plaster dust from her hands.

Her face was flushed, and her voice wavered between frustration and forced cheerfulness as she said, "That's all tidied up. But the stall holders are muttering. I might have to hide in here for the rest of the day."

At the front reception desk, Clara said into the phone, "So you acquired the picture in 1998 from an auction at Barnaby's in Bicester. Would you mind if I contacted them and used your name to see if I can discover who the vendor was?"

Gilly stood silently, watching Clara who finished the phone call with, "Thank you very much for your help."

When Clara put the phone down, Gilly said, "Sorry. That sounded important."

"Clara is researching the provenance of a painting from a house clearance last week," Dotty explained. "I thought it pleasant and worth a few hundred pounds, but Clara believes it could be worth tens of thousands. Hence the phone call."

Marion handed Dotty and Gilly mugs of tea and returned to the back of the office.

Although Dotty had understood most of the one-sided conversation, she let Clara summarise it.

Taking a mug of coffee from Marion, Clara said, "Mr Watkins sold a similar painting last year that he'd bought in 1998 at an auction house in Bicester, called Barnaby's. Do you think they'd still have the sale records?"

"Amanda Fernsby at Cirencester Auctioneers might be able to help," Dotty suggested. "Her partner, Julia Galbraith, works at Barnaby's. Why don't you give Amanda a call and see if either she'll speak to Julia for you or if she'll give you her number? Just a warning though. Julia can be rather... sharp."

Clara picked up the phone again as Gilly, Dotty, and Marion moved to the grey sofa and tub chairs in the far corner of the front reception area. They placed their mugs on drinks mats on the oval reclaimed elm coffee table.

"What exactly happened in the antique centre?" Marion asked Gilly. Both women sat in the tub chairs, facing Dotty, who sat opposite them on the sofa.

"I'm not sure exactly," Gilly admitted. "I was near the front door talking to a customer when I heard a cry and a bit of a commotion. I rushed towards the noise and saw that woman standing there, her sleek auburn hair and her rabbit fur-lined gilet covered in white plaster dust."

She started to giggle. "I know it's not funny, but you should have seen the look on her face." Then she became serious. "It wasn't amusing when one of the ceiling hooks came loose and fell to the floor, along with the basket it had been holding. We were lucky it missed the woman's friend. Do you think we'll have to remove everything from the ceiling?"

"I think that's a question for Zach. But probably," Dotty replied.

They discussed the matter for a few more minutes and then the front door opened, and Zach strode in. He removed his black raincoat and ran a hand through his dark hair. As the three women turned to look at him, Dotty felt her stomach tighten, and as Zach smiled at her, heat rose to her cheeks.

"Easy on the eye, isn't he?" murmured Marion, giving Dotty a knowing look.

Dotty's cheeks reddened even more.

"This isn't what I was expecting," Zach said.

"Have you resolved the issue without me?" He sounded both relieved and surprised.

"Marion did," Dotty replied.

"It was a team effort," Marion said modestly. "I just pointed out that plaster dust wasn't the most flattering look on social media."

Zach grinned.

"And she gave them each £100 for their inconvenience," Dotty added.

"Great work, and a potential crisis resolved," Zach said, "although it hasn't stopped the incident flying around social media with the hashtag #DustyDisaster. But at least that's not as damaging as another I saw which was #PlasteredAtAkemans."

"Oh, that's good," Gilly giggled again.

"Not really," Zach said seriously, sitting down next to Dotty.

"No, you're right, of course," Gilly conceded. "I think this is all getting too much for me."

"That's understandable," Zach said

sympathetically. "But the question is, what are we going to do about it?"

He had plenty of suggestions, most of which Gilly rejected due to the cost.

Finally, Marion said, "We're getting nowhere. I agree with Zach that we need a permanent solution, but until then, you should move the stalls closest to the wall and rope off the area to prevent anything else falling on visitors."

"But where am I going to put them?" Gilly demanded, her voice rising, edged with panic.

They all fell silent.

Then Dotty suggested, "What about in the auction room? It's not ideal, but we have space, and there's no auction this month."

"That's not a bad idea. Although I think you'd have to give them the space rent-free," Zach said, nodding. "But it won't be easy for you two and Clara, trying to work with people coming and going."

Clara approached them and said thoughtfully, "Can we move to the small auction room at the back of the main one? Just temporarily. That way, we'll be out of the way, and you can put some stalls in this space as well to draw people through to the auction room."

"That's an excellent suggestion," Zach acknowledged.

"But how much will that cost?" Gilly asked, sounding exasperated.

"Not a huge amount," Zach estimated. "It might take me a day or two to organise the power, reconnect your internet, and set up your systems, but it's doable."

"And the furniture?" Gilly pressed.

"I'll get a couple of guys to help move it. Besides, it'll give you more space. I've been wondering how the three of you manage hot-desking between two desks."

Dotty considered the suggestion and then added, "We need to finalise the auction catalogue, so we could work out of Cirencester Auctioneers for the next few days while you sort everything out."

"Then that's agreed," Zach declared.

Dotty, Marion, and Clara looked satisfied, but Gilly's shoulders slumped. "But what if people don't want to move? Or they say they're leaving? What do I do?"

"We have a client meeting tomorrow, but if Dotty's happy for me to attend that while she and Clara work on this month's auction, then afterwards I'll help you sort things out here," Marion said. "But we must remember, this is only a temporary solution."

"Agreed," Zach said. "And whatever you say, Gilly, we need to find the money. But..." He stood, opened the door into the auction house, and stepped inside.

Dotty watched as he looked around, then turned back and said, "I have a few ideas. Towards the end of the week, I'll sit down with you, your father, and Aunt Beanie to have a serious discussion."

Gilly looked relieved, probably because someone else was finally taking on the burden. For too long, she'd tried to manage the antique centre and auction house by herself.

"And I have more news about the painting," Clara said.

Zach stepped back into the office and shut the door, keeping the cold air out.

"Tell us," Marion encouraged.

"I spoke to a very helpful assistant at Barnaby's in Bicester. Because I had the name of the buyer and the year it was sold, he quickly found the entry. The painting was submitted by a Walter Jameson. But the interesting part was a note saying his daughter, Hayley, brought it to a valuation day. When asked where it had come from, she said her father acquired it during the war."

"Anything else?" Dotty asked hopefully.

"They were surprised at its value and entered it into the next auction, where it sold for £16,000. That's just over £31,000 in today's money."

"I meant anything about the seller's background?" Dotty pressed. "Although that's a sizeable sum."

"I have an address in Manchester for Walter Jameson, but if he was in the war, I doubt he's still alive."

Dotty thought about the painting, the war, and Dr Hugo Marston's face popped into her mind.

"If the address leads nowhere, I might know someone you can talk to. A specialist in artefacts taken during conflicts," she said.

"Thanks," Clara replied brightly.

Zach glanced at Gilly and Marion, determination in his tone as he said, "And now, it's time to start sorting out these stalls."

CHAPTER THIRTEEN

KEYA

Keya drove straight to the crime scene at The Owl's Nook on Monday morning. As usual, the Waterwheel Café was closed after opening over the weekend.

Through the rain, she noticed a blackboard standing at the entrance to the car park. Most of the writing had run, but it looked like someone had written a notice to say the bookshop was closed.

After parking beside a police car, she grabbed her bag and made a dash for the building's stone entrance, where a battered blue sign warned,

'Police. Stop.' It hadn't been practical to string police tape across the doorway since they needed regular access to the shop.

In the porch, she pulled on her forensic paper suit and secured booties over her damp trainers before entering the bookshop.

All was quiet inside. She planned to re-examine the area where the body had been found and work outwards from there. Even though this investigation didn't have the budget to analyse every piece of forensic evidence, it was vital to record and collect as much as possible.

The floor was cleaner than she'd expected and when she leaned on a shelf, it moved slightly, startling her. On closer inspection, she discovered the entire unit was on wheels. How clever.

She wondered where Dotty and Zach had sat during the talk they'd attended. Perhaps the shelves had been moved to make room for chairs, which would also explain the lack of dust beneath them.

There were levers at each end of this particular shelving unit. One was already raised, accounting for its instability, while the other wasn't. She pushed the second lever up and gave the shelf a careful shove. Although heavy, it glided easily across the polished wooden floorboards. And where it had stood, something glinted in the light.

Beside the area where the body had lain, she bent down and picked up a broken gold chain. Had Helen been wearing it, or had she grabbed it off her attacker during a struggle?

This was an important piece of evidence, and one she would prioritise for fingerprint and fibre analysis. She also made a note to check whether Helen had been wearing a necklace when her body was removed.

This was an excellent start to the morning.

Keya continued her investigation of the area immediately around where the body had been found. She worked systematically from the floor upwards, inspecting the nearby shelves.

The books closest to the body were historical mysteries. Adjacent to them was a section on sociology, and the rest of the shelf was dedicated to religion and spirituality.

Partway up, a white book cover caught her attention. Its bold red title read *The Denial of Death* by Ernest Becker. Keya let out a low grunt. There was no denying a death had occurred here.

"Morning," said a cheerful voice, interrupting her concentration.

She turned to see Warren who was wearing his uniform of a dark blue shirt, black trousers and a reflective stab vest with 'POLICE' printed across the chest. His radio was clipped to his shoulder.

"I saw the car and thought you must be here. Is Lynn with you?" Keya asked.

"She's talking to the family," Warren replied. "Part interviewing, part comforting them. But we're not learning much new. What about you?"

Keya held up the transparent plastic evidence bag containing the broken gold chain.

"I found this under a shelf near where the body was discovered. Would you mind checking if our victim was wearing a necklace when she was admitted to the mortuary?"

"Sure," Warren said, looking pleased to have something to do. He took the bag and left.

Having completed her re-examination of the area around where the body had been found, Keya decided she needed a break and removed her forensic suit. Exploring the rest of the property might stretch the limits of her role as crime scene manager, but it did give her an opportunity to indulge in some investigative work.

She pushed open a door at the far end of the bookshop and found herself in a large but inviting café space. Tables and chairs were arranged between low bookshelves, along with occasional tables stacked with books. More bookshelves lined the walls.

She smiled at the furniture, which was similar to that in her own cafe, being a mixture of vintage and period pieces that suited the bookish atmosphere perfectly.

A fireplace on the far wall drew her attention. Its grate was filled with ash, and a neat pile of logs was arranged beside it, suggesting it was often lit on colder days to keep the cafe snug.

A few sofas and small armchairs were scattered around, creating a pleasant environment for relaxing with a book or enjoying a quiet moment.

The ceiling was high, with exposed wooden rafters giving the room a rustic charm. At one end, a large arched window stretched nearly to the ceiling, though on this dreary April day, little light filtered through its rain-streaked panes.

Keya began at the window end and worked methodically through the café space, checking for anything out of place.

She knew she couldn't conduct a thorough search on her own, but since this area hadn't been the primary crime scene, her aim was to spot anything unusual, or that didn't belong, or that might have been moved during the incident.

At the far end of the room, near the counter and kitchen area, she found another door. The handle turned easily in her hand, and she opened it to reveal a small cupboard inside. As expected, there were boxes of books stacked neatly, but what immediately caught her eye was an old, dented metal chest.

It was a faded green colour, with the words Lt. F. Tyndall, 3rd Infantry painted in black. Discoloured stickers adorned its surface, their lettering too worn to read. As she stepped closer, she noticed an etched image of a bird, perhaps an owl, which seemed fitting given the bookshop's name.

Keya hesitated, knowing this was unlikely to be directly related to the crime. But as part of the investigation…

She crouched down and undid the metal clasps securing the lid. She lifted it open to reveal an assortment of vintage military items, including a soldier's cap and belt.

On top of the contents was a modern brown-backed scrapbook. She opened it carefully, revealing pencil sketches inside. Flipping through the pages, she saw whimsical doodles of owls alongside more detailed drawings.

There were sketches of landscapes and villages, and one depicted a grand house. Two drawings near the back seemed out of place. The first appeared to show a collection of antiques and paintings, while the other was of a single ornate cup with a wide top, narrow middle, and rounded base.

Tucked beneath the scrapbook was a small wooden box, its lid engraved with a tree and lettering Keya didn't recognise. The box shimmered faintly as mother-of-pearl inlays caught the light. She carried it out of the cupboard and placed it on the cafe counter, carefully lifting the lid.

Inside, two photographs immediately drew her attention. One was of a young man in military attire, and the other showed six men, also in uniform. The house in the background of the group photograph looked remarkably like the one sketched in the scrapbook.

Other items in the box included a tarnished circular medal with a faded red, white, and blue ribbon, a metal medallion bearing a swastika, and a small piece of cloth with an owl drawn in chalk. So many owls, Keya thought.

"What are you doing?" a sharp voice demanded, making Keya jump.

She guiltily dropped the medallion back into the box and turned to see a girl in her late teens standing in the doorway.

“Those are my Great-Grandad’s wartime things,” the girl said accusingly. “You’ve no business rooting through them.”

Keya straightened, trying to keep her voice calm but firm. “Actually, as the crime scene manager, I have every right. And you are?”

“Beth Fletcher. My Gran is the one who died.”

Beth wore a baggy hoodie and grey jogging bottoms. She glanced down at the floor, and Keya hoped she wasn’t about to burst into tears. Technically, Beth shouldn’t be in the room, but Keya was intrigued to know more about her and the contents of the chest.

“I’m so sorry,” Keya said sympathetically. “It’s part of my job to investigate what happened. But you say these belonged to your great-grandfather, and he fought in the war?”

“That’s right. I only found the trunk a few months ago. Gran brought it here when she moved from Guildford, but she hadn’t looked at it for years. Neither had Mum. I’ve been going through it, trying to learn more about my Great-Grandad and what he did in the war.”

"That sounds fascinating," Keya said. "And I can't help but notice all the owls. On this cloth…" She held up the piece with the chalk drawing. "And in the sketches. Is that why your grandmother named the bookshop The Owl's Nook?"

Beth's expression softened. "Her dad used to tell her stories about the war. Nothing gruesome, just things that happened near the end when he was leading a small unit. They had a young boy from Czechoslovakia assigned to them as an interpreter, that's the Czech Republic now. He had amazing instincts, and Great-Grandad joked that he could see in the dark, so they nicknamed him The Little Owl. The name stuck, and that's what they called their unit. That's why there's an owl on that cloth."

"What a lovely story," Keya said warmly. "And naming the bookshop in his memory was such a thoughtful way to honour him. But now, I'm afraid you really shouldn't be here. This area is technically part of the crime scene."

"Can I just grab a book?" Beth asked, her face falling.

"Any book in particular?" There were so many in the room.

"Something from the military history section. Most of the books in here are second-hand. The fiction ones can be swapped, but the non-fiction ones, especially the military books, are more valuable. Gran started that section with Great-Grandad's collection."

Keya nodded. "All right, go ahead."

She watched as Beth went to a shelf along the wall leading into the main bookshop, pulled out two books and returned, hesitating.

"Is there something else?" Keya asked gently.

"This might sound a bit harsh, but when can we get Gran's things back?"

"Is there something specific you'd like? To remember her by?"

Beth nodded. "There's a pendant I found in that box. Gran borrowed it but I'd really like it back."

Keya's voice softened. "All the items will need to be kept as evidence for now. But once the case is closed, I'll see what I can do."

“Thanks,” Beth said quietly before leaving.

Keya returned the box to the chest, ensuring everything was secure, and closed the cupboard door. She passed back through the cafe but as she stepped into the bookshop, a man entered through the front entrance.

Quickening her pace, she called firmly, “Hey, you can’t be in here!”

CHAPTER FOURTEEN

KEYA

Keya strode across the bookshop towards the entrance, where a scruffy-looking man in his forties was standing. At first, he appeared confused, but his expression quickly shifted to one of defiance.

"I don't know who you are or what she's told you, but I have every right to be here," he stated.

"Sir, this is a crime scene," Keya replied firmly.

"What crime?"

"There's been a death. Let's move into the entrance porch, away from the main bookshop."

Technically, Keya should have escorted the man outside, but with the rain still falling, she had no desire to get wet. More importantly, she wanted to find out who he was, what he knew, and, most intriguingly, who the 'she' was that he'd mentioned.

When she moved to place a hand on his arm to guide him out, he stepped back sharply. "Oh no, you don't. And you can't fob me off that easily. A death? Who are you trying to kid? That's a piece of fiction if I ever heard one."

"Sir, did you not see the large police sign at the entrance?" Keya asked, keeping her voice calm.

"For show," he scoffed. "Come on, where is she? Just because she knows I'm coming doesn't mean she has to send the hired help to pretend to be a police officer."

"She doesn't need to pretend," said Warren as he stepped through the porch and came to stand beside the man. "She is."

Keya suppressed a wry smile. Or was, she thought.

"And so am I," Warren added, his tone steady. "Constable Warren Sparrow. And you are, sir?"

The man squared his shoulders and replied, "Declan Reid. And I'm family."

Keya's eyebrows rose slightly in surprise, but Warren's expression remained impassive. "And how are you related to the victim, Helen Fletcher?" Warren asked.

"Helen, a victim?" Declan laughed, although it sounded hollow.

"Sir, this is not a laughing matter. Helen Fletcher was found dead in the bookshop on Saturday evening."

Declan tugged at the collar of his faded leather jacket, his expression turning to one of surprise. "You're not joking, are you? Is that why you're here? To investigate Helen's death?"

"Yes, sir. Now, please tell me your full name and your relationship to the victim."

Declan straightened his back and ran a hand over his thinning hair. "The victim? She was my mother-in-law. My name's Declan Reid."

"So you were married to Laura?" Keya asked, guessing at the relationship.

"Laura is—was—my wife. And Elizabeth my daughter."

"And your current address?" Warren prompted, notebook and pen ready.

"Ah, well, that's a tricky one," Declan said evasively. "I'm staying with a friend at the moment."

"And their address?" Warren asked, his tone weary.

Declan hesitated, then reluctantly gave an address near Aldershot.

"When did you last see Helen Fletcher?" Keya enquired, watching him closely. She noticed him glance down at the floor and shift his weight before answering.

"On one of my visits to the bookshop," he said guardedly.

"And when was that?" Warren pressed, his patience impressive.

"I don't know. I don't exactly carry a diary around."

"Mr Reid," Keya said, her tone sharper. "You mentioned you're staying in Aldershot. That's a two-hour journey, isn't it?"

"Something like that," he muttered.

"So you wouldn't just pop round here. You'd have to make a special trip. Unless…" She let the suggestion hang in the air, hoping to nudge him into revealing more.

Warren shot her a questioning glance, which she ignored.

"Unless you're currently staying locally. Perhaps temporarily," she added, her tone encouraging.

Declan's expression shifted uncomfortably. "Yeah, well, it's a nice area. Lots of walks."

Keya fought the urge to roll her eyes. She doubted Declan walked anywhere except to the pub.

"What's your local address?" Warren asked, as he clutched his pen.

"The Plough, at the end of St Edward's Drive," Declan admitted grudgingly.

"And how long have you been staying there?" Warren enquired.

Declan shuffled his scuffed trainers on the polished floor before replying. "A few weeks."

Warren glanced at Keya, who gave an almost imperceptible shake of her head. They could easily verify how long Declan had been staying there from The Plough's records.

"Why are you here?" Keya asked directly. "Is it to see Beth?"

Declan avoided her gaze. "She's my daughter. I have a right to see her," he muttered defensively.

"How old is Beth?" Keya asked.

"Sixteen," Warren answered before Declan could.

"Then it's up to Beth whether she sees you or not, unless you have a court order," Keya said firmly, watching him closely.

"Well, no, nothing like that. But as I said, she is my daughter," he protested.

Keya sighed. She'd had enough of Declan's evasiveness. "Mr Reid, unless you have information relating to Helen's death, I'll have to ask you to leave the crime scene and let me get on with my work."

Declan actually looked relieved as Warren led him away. Watching him go, Keya couldn't shake a nagging unease. A sense that she'd missed something important.

But for now, her priority was finishing her work at the crime scene.

CHAPTER FIFTEEN

KEYA

An hour later, Keya heard Inspector Lynn's voice calling through the bookshop.

"Keya? Are you still here?"

Keya stepped out from behind a bookshelf and saw Lynn standing in the entrance porch.

"Do you fancy a break and a bite of lunch?" Lynn asked. "Laura recommended Lucy's Tearoom in town, and I know Warren's getting peckish."

The three of them drove into Stow-on-the-Wold and parked outside a period stone building with a prominent bay window on the ground floor and above it a sign for 'Lucy's Tearoom'.

Inside, the walls were painted a warm cream, and pretty bunting festooned the low ceiling and exposed dark wooden beams. The café was bustling, but they managed to find seats at a vintage pine table.

The atmosphere was warm and inviting, a pleasant contrast to the dreary April weather. Warren immediately picked up the paper menu while Keya glanced at the specials board. The soup of the day was pumpkin.

"Declan Reid was an unexpected visitor today," Lynn said as they settled in. "Neither Laura nor Beth mentioned his existence before, but they've now admitted they knew he was staying locally. Apparently, he's been pestering them. Laura has flat-out refused to meet him, but Beth had supper with him at the King's Arms on the Market Square last Wednesday."

"Is he a suspect?" Keya asked.

"I've added him to the list," Lynn replied.

"But I don't have a motive for him, and there's no evidence he met Helen directly, although I believe he admitted to you two that he had. We need to see if there are any messages between him and

Helen, or Helen and anyone else, for that matter. Warren can start working through her phone when we're back at the station this afternoon. Then there's her emails and online activity. Have you come across a computer yet, Keya?"

"No, not yet."

Warren looked up from his menu. "There are a couple of laptops in the house. One's definitely Beth's, but the other?"

"Remind me when we get back to ask about that," Lynn said. "If Helen used it, we'll see if we can persuade Laura to give us the password. Then one of us can go through it as that'll be quicker than sending it off for analysis."

"Good idea," Keya said, appreciating Lynn's practical approach. "And how are Laura and Beth? Is there any chance they had a grievance against Helen that escalated into violence?"

"It's possible," Lynn admitted, "but I don't think so. Beth, as you've seen, is quiet and a bit of a nerd. Not the type to rebel or have heated rows. She's not sneaking out in short skirts to meet boys late at night, that's for sure."

Keya nodded. That image didn't fit the geeky girl she'd met.

"And Laura," Lynn continued. "She and her mum have lived together happily for twelve years. They've built up the bookshop, added the cafe, and Laura works part-time as a teacher. She says it gives her some independence and a bit of a social life. It doesn't feel like there's tension there, let alone anything serious enough to lead to murder."

At that moment, a kindly, grey-haired woman approached their table. "Are you ready to order?" she asked, giving them all wary looks.

"The soup, please," said Lynn immediately, "and one of your homemade sausage rolls."

Keya wondered when Lynn had found the time to decide. She quickly looked down at the menu as Warren asked hopefully, "Can I have the classic fish finger sandwich?"

"Of course, and for you?" enquired the woman.

Keya quickly made her selection. "Lucy's rarebit, please."

"Good choice," the woman said approvingly. "And to drink?"

"Water," Lynn replied.

"Coke," said Warren.

"A pot of tea, please," Keya requested.

As the woman left, they returned to their discussion.

"So, you don't think it was Laura or Beth, and we can't tie Declan in yet. Who else is there?" Keya asked.

"Nicole Blake," Warren said immediately.

"The bookshop assistant?"

"Yes. She's right dodgy," Warren added.

"We don't know that for sure," Lynn interjected.

"But she found the body," Warren said. "That's suspicious enough. And what was she doing back at the bookshop after five on a Saturday evening if she'd been out most of the afternoon making deliveries? And how many people in Stow even get books delivered?"

"Surely you have the order details?" Keya asked.

"No, and that's also shady," Warren said, leaning back and crossing his arms.

Lynn explained, "Nicole claims her delivery schedule was handwritten, and she threw the list away after she'd finished. When we asked for computer invoices, she said there weren't any. Apparently, people either popped into the bookshop or ordered over the phone."

"I agree with Warren," Keya said. "That does sound dodgy."

"I'll make it a priority to look for those orders if we get access to the computer and business accounts," Lynn said.

"So, is Nicole your prime suspect?" Keya asked.

"By default," Lynn admitted. "But we don't have a motive. Laura and Beth said she wanted more of a managerial role in the bookshop and felt Helen didn't entirely trust her. But it sounded like normal workplace frustration, nothing more."

"What about the computer system?" Warren asked.

"There's that," Lynn said. "Nicole wanted to upgrade it, and Helen thought it was a good idea.

She asked Imogen Henshaw to review the system and the business. Beth thinks that put Nicole's nose out of joint."

"But it's hardly a motive for murder," Keya mused, as the grey-haired lady returned and gave her an alarmed look.

Giving Keya a wide berth, she set a plate and a large white bowl down in front of Lynn, who smiled warmly and said, "Thank you."

The pumpkin soup smelled rich, with a hint of nutmeg.

The cheese on Keya's rarebit bubbled invitingly, covering two crumpets, and it was accompanied by a fresh salad of green leaves.

Both Keya and Lynn stared at Warren's fish finger sandwich, which consisted of thick slices of white bread, breaded fish fingers, and what appeared to be cheese and gherkins.

Lynn dipped her spoon into her soup and concluded, "So, overall, we have no motive, no witnesses, and no solid leads. We need a break. Some evidence, a hint of a grudge, anything to help us understand why someone killed Helen."

CHAPTER SIXTEEN

DOTTY

Towards the end of Monday afternoon, Dotty decided to take a break from her work and the ongoing discussions about Akemans, its problems, and its future.

Rather than find somewhere quiet, she chose the relative anonymity of sitting at a corner table in the Waterwheel Cafe. She still overheard mentions of Akemans, but the customers soon moved on to other news and chatter.

Marion was right about one thing. People in the Cotswolds loved nothing better than a good gossip.

Dotty had brought the gold owl pendant with her, and as she sipped her floral Earl Grey tea, she held it in the palm of her hand, turning it gently. Opening her tablet, she typed in the maker's name, Otto Mond, and waited for the search results.

The first one confirmed his biographical details. Mond had emigrated to the UK in 1939 and died in 1951. He was a skilled craftsman known for custom commissions and intricate designs.

There was even a grainy photograph of Mond in his workshop, surrounded by tools. Dotty peered at it, but she couldn't make out much about the man himself except that he appeared to have dark hair, thin features, and a prominent nose.

Another result detailed an auction listing for a pair of gold earrings Mond had crafted, which had sold a few years ago for just over £2,000. But Dotty was disappointed to find that little else was recorded about him.

One description stated plainly: "Little is known about Otto Mond's commissions, as most were undocumented."

As she held the pendant up to the light, watching its eyes glint, she wondered if she'd ever discover why or for whom it had been made.

A shadow fell across the table, and when she looked up, Keya was standing there.

"More owls," Keya said, sighing. "I've had my fill of them today."

"Do you mean your crime scene?" Dotty asked. "You can hardly blame the poor owl for that. It's people, not owls, who are at fault."

"That's true," Keya admitted, pulling out a chair and slumping onto it.

"But there's the bookshop name, the wooden murder weapon, and today I found an old tin trunk. Inside were sketches of owls. One was even chalked onto a piece of cloth. Beth, the victim's granddaughter, told me they belonged to her great-grandfather. She recently discovered the trunk, and if you're interested in owl emblems, she told me a story."

"Go on," Dotty encouraged, intrigued.

"Her great-grandad used to tell our victim Helen, his daughter, stories from the end of the war.

Apparently, he was in charge of a small team that included an interpreter. Because of his skill at keeping them out of trouble, they nicknamed him The Little Owl. And that became the name of their unit."

Dotty held the pendant up again as she considered Keya's words and remembered what Helen had said after Dr Marston's talk.

After a pause, she spoke. "There are some similarities between your case and my house clearance."

"Really?" Keya sounded surprised.

"They both have connections to the Second World War. My client had military history books and comics, and I think he was a soldier."

Keya frowned. "I don't see how being interested in the war connects to our investigation. And you don't know for certain he served."

"No, but given his age, it's likely he did. He was ninety-eight when he died. And a lot of men of that generation didn't just read about the war, they lived it."

"Okay, that makes sense. And I accept that my victim's father also fought. I think his name was Lieutenant Francis Tyndall, or at least that was printed on the old trunk I found. But many men of his generation served. Isn't the link a little tenuous?"

"Then there are the owl pendants," Dotty said. "This one," she added, holding up Pete's pendant, which she had been playing with, "and a similar one I spotted your victim wearing the night Zach and I met her at the literary festival."

"She wasn't wearing one when she died," Keya replied. "Warren checked, and there was no necklace." Her voice trailed off, and Dotty could see her thinking. After a moment, she added, "That's why I asked him about it. Because I found a broken gold chain near the body."

"I'm certain Helen was wearing something like this," Dotty said, placing the gold owl pendant in Keya's hand.

Keya weighed it in her palm. "Do you think someone took it?"

"It's possible, if you didn't find it at the crime scene."

Keya nodded. "This could be important. I'd better go back and search for it tomorrow. I wonder if Warren is free to help me. If our assailant grabbed the necklace and the pendant went flying, it could've slid a long way across the polished floorboards."

"More likely, it's stuck in a book," Dotty considered.

"Oh, no. There are thousands of those. It'll take me the rest of the week to check them all."

"I'm sorry to add to your workload," Dotty apologised.

"Don't worry," Keya said, smiling. "Lynn said we need a break in the case, and this might be it." She handed the owl pendant back. "What do you know about it?"

"Apart from the name of the jeweller and that it was made before he died in 1951, not much. There's no official gold hallmark, so it's unregistered, which makes it harder to trace."

"But you'll try, while I look for the other one?" Keya suggested.

"Yes," Dotty replied hesitantly, "although Clara and I will be working at Cirencester Auctioneers for the next few days. Did you hear what happened?"

Dotty recounted the morning's events, including the woman who was covered in plaster and the video of her going viral on social media. Then she described her suggestion to use the auction house space, and Clara's idea for moving the office.

"Zach says it'll take a few days to get everything sorted. And since we need to work on the auction catalogue, we might as well do so in situ as we're holding this month's auction at Cirencester Auctioneers."

"Thank goodness for Zach and his practical approach," Keya agreed.

"And Marion has a level head on her shoulders. I'm not sure we'd have managed to calm Gilly down and deal with everything so quickly without her. But," Dotty added, "this is just a temporary solution. I'm relying on Zach to find us a permanent one."

CHAPTER SEVENTEEN

DOTTY

On Tuesday morning, Clara and Dotty worked at Cirencester Auctioneers as planned. The weather remained grey, although thankfully there was no rain.

Dotty parked outside what had once been a large aircraft hangar for Cotswold Airport during its days as a military base.

The double-height building, constructed of stone with solid corner columns and a curved, black-tiled roof, still had an imposing presence on the industrial estate which had built up around it.

Dotty collected her bag and basket from the car and walked towards the main entrance, set in the middle of one of the building's long frontages between four oversized metal casement windows. The once-bright flower beds beneath the windows were now overrun with weeds, and the peeling paint on the door frame gave the place a neglected air.

Inside, Dotty's mood brightened. The freestanding shelves nearest the door were stacked with boxes of items. Individually, they weren't worth much, but they had been bundled together for the sale, and there were plenty of them.

There was also the usual mismatched collection of furniture near the auctioneer's raised rostrum, including old chairs for customers to sit on. To the right, Dotty noticed more furniture and some unusual items, such as a vintage butcher's delivery bicycle and a gothic metal garden arch.

That was the charm of auctions. The sheer variety of items put up for sale, each one waiting to find a new home. It felt far more rewarding than simply throwing things away.

The auction office was located in the ground floor of an internal breeze-block structure. Above it were more showrooms, which were rarely used, and a small cafe that opened only on auction days.

As Dotty stepped inside, Amanda looked up from the large desk at the far end and smiled warmly. Her golden-brown hair was neatly tied back in a ponytail, and she was wearing a padded gilet over a baggy green jumper.

"It's great to have some company," Amanda said. "Is Clara joining us too?"

"Yes," Dotty replied as she placed her bag and basket on a desk. She had a choice of several but chose one close to Amanda.

"I'm sorry to hear about the trouble at Akemans, but that video of the woman getting covered in plaster was very funny," Amanda said, her amber eyes sparkling with amusement.

"I suppose it was," Dotty admitted, "but it's also incredibly frustrating. Zach and I keep saying something needs to be done, but…" She trailed off, not wanting to speak ill of Gilly or her father.

Amanda gave her a knowing look. "There's no money for it, I assume? I get it. This place is draining me too. That's why I'm so glad you're combining your auction with ours again."

"We're grateful too," Dotty said, "but it's not a long-term solution. The fewer auctions we hold on-site, the more our business suffers."

Amanda nodded thoughtfully. "That makes sense. Ah, and here's Clara."

For the next couple of hours, the three women worked quietly. Dotty left Clara and Amanda to focus on the catalogue while she created condition reports in the main auction area. Occasionally, Clara emerged from the office to check an item or take more photographs.

They continued working steadily through Tuesday, making significant progress on the auction catalogue. By late Wednesday morning, Amanda finally announced, "We're done. That's the catalogue sent to the printers."

Dotty, who had been typing up a condition report for a Georgian oak tallboy, stood and stretched. "That calls for a cuppa."

As Amanda set the kettle to boil, she asked, "How many more condition reports do we need?"

Dotty checked her list. “I’m about halfway through.”

“In that case, why don’t I take over for a bit, so you can catch up on Akemans’ work?” Amanda suggested.

“Thanks. I should check my emails. Clara, what about you?”

“I still need to go through Pete Reynolds’ paperwork,” Clara replied.

Once they had their hot drinks, they settled back at their desks. Dotty decided, after Clara had mentioned Pete Reynolds, that her first task should be to contact Dr Hugo Marston.

She’d noted his details during his talk, so she composed an email outlining the discovery of Pete’s painting and its potential link to one that had supposedly been acquired during the Second World War. For good measure, she attached several photos Clara had taken for the auction catalogue.

After sending the email, she checked her inbox. There was nothing urgent, so she turned her attention to researching the owl pendant. She wasn't hopeful about uncovering much, but the more she thought about it, the more convinced she became that it was connected to Keya's case.

If her work could help both Akemans and the investigation, it was worth the effort.

She had just clicked on what felt like the hundredth auction listing for a gold owl pendant when her phone rang. The number was unfamiliar. She took a deep breath, preparing for either a complaining customer or an opportunistic journalist, and answered.

"Hello, is that Dotty Sayers?" a pleasant male voice asked.

"Yes, it is," Dotty replied steadily.

"This is Hugo Marston. I've just read your very interesting email."

"Oh! I wasn't expecting such a quick response."

"I always enjoy hearing about newly discovered pieces. What an intriguing little painting. You mentioned the war in your email, and I presume you're wondering if it might be something the Nazis stole. I'd say it's unlikely, but I do know several of Josef Stoitzner's works went missing at the end of the war."

"Clara, who's been researching the painting, traced the other one I mentioned in my email back to a Walter Jameson, who sold it at Barnaby's auction house in 1998."

"That's excellent information," Hugo said, the sound of typing in the background. "I'd love to dig into this for you, but as you may know, the International Art Recovery Alliance isn't a charity. We do charge a fee for our services."

Dotty hesitated. "How much are we talking about?"

"The initial work would be around £1,000. If it proves promising, it could go up to £3,000 or £5,000 at most, depending on the depth of research needed. However, with provenance, the painting's value could increase significantly."

Dotty considered this. "It's our liability, though. The client's only interested in the end result."

"I understand. But why don't I start with the initial work, and we can reassess from there?"

"OK," Dotty agreed reluctantly. Perhaps she could justify deducting the cost from the end price. On a whim, she added, "This might be totally unrelated, but when we found the painting, a small gold owl pendant was hanging from it."

"Send me the details and a photo," Hugo suggested. "I'll see if there's any connection."

After they ended the call, Amanda looked over and said, "That sounded promising."

Dotty explained the situation, and Clara chimed in with her research findings. "So, Dr Marston will investigate the painting for us," Dotty concluded.

"That's exciting," Amanda said. "Imagine if it's been hidden, or at least hanging in this Pete's house since the war, with nobody else knowing of its existence. Sometimes I really do love this job."

CHAPTER EIGHTEEN

DOTTY

Dotty sat in the ground-floor office at Cirencester Auctioneers with Amanda Fernsby, who ran the auction company. Clara, Akemans' receptionist and, as Dotty now thought of her, an antique apprentice, was with them.

Dotty was answering an email from a potential client when Clara said in a sceptical voice, "This is strange."

"What is?" Dotty asked.

Amanda was also staring at Clara.

"I've been going through the paperwork you brought back from Pete Reynolds' house. There's a file of old black-and-white photographs, letters, papers, and Pete's discharge documents from the military. There's also another file of newspaper clippings. But the recent paperwork is mostly letters and notes between him and someone called Beth. They're discussing the war and his experiences, and there are several mentions of Little Owls…"

"Really?" remarked Dotty, sitting up straighter and giving Clara her full attention.

"But this is the most interesting document, as far as we're concerned." Clara held up a piece of paper.

"A letter, dated the beginning of December last year, signed by Pete and two witnesses. It bequeaths the pendant and painting to an Elizabeth Fletcher."

Clara looked proudly at Dotty and Amanda, her eyes shining.

"Elizabeth… Beth," Dotty mused. "Beth Fletcher. Helen Fletcher. Little Owls. That can't be a coincidence, surely. And I told Keya Pete was a soldier. Is there any mention of a Lieutenant Francis Tyndall in the correspondence?"

"Oh, yes. He was the leader of their unit, The Little Owls."

"I knew there was a link," said Dotty in a satisfied tone.

"A link with what?" Amanda asked.

"The death at my friend Keya's crime scene. The deceased is Helen Fletcher, daughter of Francis Tyndall and grandmother of Elizabeth—Beth—Fletcher."

"So," Clara said thoughtfully, "Pete was corresponding with Beth about his experiences in the Second World War, and then he left her his two most treasured possessions."

"Yes. And I wonder how they first met? Probably at the bookshop." Dotty answered her own question.

"Both Zach and Beth told me it's known for its collection of second-hand military books. Perhaps Pete went to look through them and got talking to Beth. Maybe he already knew who she was, or perhaps that only came out during their conversations."

"How old is Beth?" Amanda asked.

"Sixteen."

"Isn't it a bit odd for her to be talking to an old man like this Pete? And about the Second World War?"

"Not after she found her great-grandfather's trunk of military and war memorabilia. Having met her, I think she'd be keen to know more."

"So she and Pete struck up a friendship based on their mutual interest in the war," Clara concluded, "and Pete left her those items."

Clearly, the bequest was the most important aspect for Clara, but Dotty was more intrigued by the link between Pete, Beth, and ultimately Helen.

Had Pete told Beth something that led to Helen's death? And how had Pete himself died? Or was she just getting carried away? Dotty shook her head, trying to clear her thoughts.

"Are you all right?" Amanda asked.

"My sleuthing tendencies sometimes lead me down theoretical rabbit holes," Dotty admitted, "and I start thinking everyone's a suspect and every death is a murder."

"Oh dear," Amanda said with a laugh. "I hope you don't think I'm going to turn around and stab you both. But I do think we should call it a day. We've done some good work. Are you here tomorrow, or back at Akemans?"

"Akemans, I think. Zach said they moved the furniture this morning, and he was going to connect the systems this afternoon. I might go and see how he's getting on."

"What about this letter, and the other paperwork?" Clara asked, sounding concerned.

"I'll take that too. I'll need to give a copy of the letter to Pete's nephew. He won't be happy to find out the only really valuable assets of the estate have been given to someone else. And I need to discuss the discovery of the letter with Keya."

When Dotty returned to Akemans, she found Zach in the smaller auction room at the back of the main one, and she gasped at the transformation. The metal frames used to display paintings and pictures had been removed, and the walls were now painted a light grey.

The glass display cabinets, used for jewellery and other small valuables, were gone. In their place were four desks, several cupboards, and some bookshelves.

At the back of the room, a table held a kettle, mugs, and all the essentials for making hot drinks. The layout even included space for the grey sofa, matching chairs, and the elm coffee table from the reception area.

It was a remarkable change, making the space feel both professional and welcoming.

"What do you think?" Zach asked, looking up from the far desk where he'd been tapping at a computer keyboard.

"It looks good. No, better than that. Fantastic. When did you have time to paint?"

"I tasked the guys who moved the furniture to do it yesterday. The walls were in a bit of a state after we removed the metal framework."

"And four desks?" Dotty enquired, raising an eyebrow.

"I thought you might need an extra one," Zach admitted, his ears turning pink as he focused on the computer monitor. "I should have the systems connected in half an hour."

"Then why don't I meet you in the cafe? I need to chat with Keya about her case first anyway."

Zach looked up and grinned. "Are you sleuthing again?"

"No," Dotty said defensively. "But Clara found some papers from one of our house clearances which might be connected to her case."

Zach's grin widened indulgently as Dotty turned and left the office space.

As she walked through the antique centre, she noticed the yellow cordon and the empty stalls closest to the shared wall with the auction house. She presumed the stalls would be moved the next day.

Inside the cafe, she found Keya sitting at a table, staring intently at a laptop screen.

"Police or cafe work?" Dotty asked as she sat down opposite her friend.

"Police. Lynn's shared her investigation files with me, and Warren's just added a note on Declan

Reid. He's Laura's ex-husband and he's been staying in Stow-on-the-Wold for the past three weeks. The address he gave for a friend he was staying with checks out, but apparently, he's not welcome back. Something about money. And he has a criminal record."

"For what?" Dotty asked.

"Various things. He's been in and out of prison for loan scams, insurance fraud, and selling fake goods. You know the type."

Dotty nodded. "But nothing violent?" she asked.

"No, that doesn't seem to be his usual remit. But it doesn't mean he couldn't be provoked."

"True. But I've got something else for you, and for Lynn."

"Oh?" Keya looked at her expectantly.

"You know our house clearance?"

"The one where you found the gold owl?"

"Yes," Dotty confirmed. "Clara was going through the owner's papers and found this." She placed the bequest letter on the table.

Keya started reading, then stopped, her mouth forming a silent O as she shot a look at Dotty before returning to the letter.

When she finished, she asked, "Who exactly was Peter Reynolds?"

"I don't know much. We were instructed by his nephew, who doesn't seem particularly interested in Pete's things except for what they are worth."

"Then he might be disappointed," Keya said, tapping the letter.

"There are some comics, a few first edition books and an attractive desk, but those items in the letter are likely to be the most valuable parts of his estate. As for Pete, I was wondering if you, Lynn or Warren could look into his death."

"You don't think it was suspicious, do you?"

"No, he was ninety-eight, but still…"

"His connection to Beth, and through her to Helen, raises questions?"

"It does to me," Dotty agreed.

"OK," Keya said with a nod. "Let me see what I can find out."

CHAPTER NINETEEN

KEYA

On Thursday morning, Keya drove to The Owl's Nook. This really was the last time, she told herself.

If she didn't find the pendant today, the one Dotty was so adamant Helen had been wearing, then it simply wasn't there to be found. Maybe Helen hadn't had it on when she died after all.

The lab had found nothing useful on the gold chain. The links were too small to hold fingerprints, and there were no fibres, hairs, or anything else of use.

In fact, there was nothing to prove Helen had even worn it. Someone else might have dropped it near the shelf, and a stray foot or a brush had swept it underneath until Keya had come across it.

As she turned into the bookshop's gravel car park, her phone rang. It was Warren.

"Morning," she said wearily.

Warren didn't react to her tone but instead said, "I'll be a bit late this morning. I have a few things to check regarding Peter Reynolds' death."

"It doesn't look suspicious, does it?" she asked.

"No, not on the face of it. He died in hospital, but it's the circumstances that put him there which might be of interest."

"Why?" Keya straightened, her weariness replaced by curiosity.

"I'll tell you when I see you," Warren replied evasively and then hung up.

Inside the bookshop, Keya began her search for the pendant in the romance section. Nothing.

Next, she moved to children's literature. She picked up *Treasure Island* by Robert Louis Stevenson and gave it a shake.

No hidden treasure this time. But then, as she reached for the aptly named *The Owl and the Pussycat*, she saw something glint in the light.

Was it really the pendant she'd been looking for? Carefully, she removed the thin illustrated hardback edition of the book. And there, wedged between the top edges of the covers, was a small gold owl with one blue and one white eye.

"Gotcha!" she murmured triumphantly.

She thought she heard a car crunching on the gravel outside, so she dropped the pendant into a transparent evidence bag and walked across to the front porch. Warren would be relieved the search was over.

But when she opened the solid wooden front door, she saw Dotty climbing out of her chic little car.

"Hi," Dotty called.

"What are you doing here?" Keya asked in a puzzled tone.

Walking towards her, Dotty replied, "I spoke to our lawyers this morning about the bequest letter we found in Pete Reynolds' papers. We agreed the nephew won't be happy. I chickened out of calling him and sent an email instead, but the lawyer believes the letter is legal. I sent him a copy to check and brought another one for Beth. If the painting and owl pendant are hers, I'll need her permission to continue our research, especially since the cost will fall on her. How are you getting on?"

Keya held up the small evidence bag and, in a triumphant voice, exclaimed, "I've found it!"

"Oh! Helen's pendant. Can I see it?"

"Sure." Keya handed the bag to Dotty, who held it in her palm as she examined the contents.

"It's not identical to Pete's. The eyes are different, for a start. The stones in his are red and amber. Look, this one is sitting on a branch. Pete's isn't. I wonder what that represents?"

"Probably nothing," Keya replied. "The jeweller likely gave each one a little twist to make it unique."

"I'm sure you're right," Dotty agreed. She was about to hand the bag back when a mischievous look crossed her face.

"What is it?" asked Keya warily.

"Well, I need to speak to Beth and her mother about the bequest. I'm sure Beth, in particular, will be pleased you've found the owl."

"Oh, she will," agreed Keya. "She asked me about a pendant at the start of the week."

"Then why don't you come with me? You can ask them to confirm it's the one Helen was wearing."

"I don't think that's in doubt," Keya protested.

"I know," Dotty said evenly, "but showing it to her gives us a chance to ask questions."

Keya realised where Dotty was going with this. "Of course," she agreed. After all, part of her role was to identify the evidence she found, and Lynn wanted her help with the investigation. "Come with me. We'll use the side door."

Laura and Helen lived in a two-storey brick building attached to the rear of the bookshop and cafe.

"Hiya!" Keya called after she knocked and opened the door.

"That's not how we usually do it," she heard a

slightly petulant female voice say. It sounded like Nicole.

A more polished voice responded, “Exactly. That’s why I’m here. To look at updating your system and move it forward to meet the modern needs of bookshops.”

“Is that Imogen Henshaw?” whispered Dotty.

Keya thought it was, but before she could answer, Laura Fletcher walked down the narrow coir-matted corridor towards them.

From the few times she’d met Laura, Keya thought of her as practical and approachable. Today, she was wearing a lightweight navy gilet over a long-sleeved grey t-shirt, paired with a scarf and dark denim jeans.

“Hello, Keya. And you’ve brought a friend. Have we met before?” Laura asked warmly, looking at Dotty.

“I attended the talk last week given by Dr Marston.”

“Of course, you were with Zach. Please come through to the living room,” Laura invited.

They followed her. As Laura turned into a room on their right, Keya glanced through an open doorway opposite and saw Imogen Henshaw sitting at a desk with a laptop. Beside her, Nicole sat on a wooden kitchen chair, her mouth drawn into a thin line.

Turning back to Laura, Keya asked, her voice tinged with surprise, "You know Zach?"

"Oh, yes. He's been quite a regular at the bookshop. He enjoys sitting in the cafe with a book and a cup of coffee. And sometimes he stays for lunch," Laura replied, gesturing to a faded yellow sofa.

"What sort of books?" Keya asked, intrigued.

"Probably military history. He's looking into his heritage again," Dotty acknowledged.

"Yes, that, but lately he's been going through books on antiques and collectibles."

"Has he now?" Keya grinned and glanced at Dotty. "I wonder why?"

Dotty's cheeks flushed, and she stammered, "I work for Akemans. At the auction house."

"I don't think there's anything of my mother's we intend to sell," Laura said practically, motioning for them to sit.

"Oh, that's not why I'm here," Dotty said quickly. "I have some news for Beth."

"Beth?"

"Yes. Does the name Pete, or Peter, Reynolds mean anything to you?"

Laura's face softened. "Pete was a lovely old man. He became a regular at the bookshop and cafe. I often gave him lunch for free or at cost. I don't think he had much money. He died in January after falling at a charity event. It was such a shame. Helen attended his funeral. And he'd been helping Beth research her great-grandfather. But you'll have to ask her about that."

"Is she here?" Dotty asked.

"Yes, in her bedroom. Shall I fetch her?"

"Yes, please," Dotty replied.

When Laura left, Dotty turned to Keya and suggested, "You should tell her about the owl pendant first."

“OK,” Keya agreed.

From the room opposite, they heard Imogen say, “This is strange. It looks like some files have been deleted. Let me see if I can recover them.”

“Is that necessary?” asked Nicole. “We’re supposed to be creating a new system, not digging through the old one.”

“It might be a bug,” protested Imogen, “or something we need to consider while making updates.”

“I really don’t think this is what Helen wanted,” Nicole said defensively.

“What isn’t?” asked Laura, reappearing in the doorway as Beth entered the sitting room and sat down on a small, straight-backed chair with a large white cushion featuring an owl.

“I just meant,” Nicole began, her voice sounding level but with a hint of strain, “that Helen asked Imogen to create a solution to help with more online orders, and a new marketing strategy for customers who don’t want to visit the bookshop in person. I don’t think she should be digging into old files, whether they’re missing or not.”

"I think Helen wanted Imogen to overhaul everything and, for that, she'll need to assess the current state of things," Laura responded in a placatory tone.

"But..." Nicole protested.

"Nicole, why don't you let Imogen get on with it? We've had several deliveries of new books, and even though we can't get into the shop at the moment …" Laura turned and gave Keya a quick glance. "We can at least match them with existing orders and get those dispatched."

A sullen-looking Nicole stomped out of the room opposite and turned into the corridor.

"Sorry about that," Laura apologised to Imogen. "Nicole gets rather territorial about how things are run in the bookshop. I don't know why. It's not as if we have anything to hide."

Laura entered the sitting room and sat down just as Beth said, "You wanted to see me?"

"Yes, Dotty does, but first I wanted to show you this," Keya said, holding up the transparent evidence bag.

"The owl pendant! You found it?" Beth exclaimed.

"Yes, and I'd like you to confirm if it's the one Helen, your grandmother, was wearing the day she died."

Beth held out her hand, and Keya handed her the bag.

"Oh, yes," Beth said, examining it. "I know this is my great-grandfather's. I found it in a box in his trunk. It's different from the others. They all have different coloured eyes, but this owl is perched on a branch."

"What others?" chorused Keya and Dotty together.

CHAPTER TWENTY

DOTTY

Dotty watched as Beth continued to examine the small owl pendant Keya had found in the bookshop, which Beth had identified as belonging to her great-grandfather.

"So can you confirm," asked Keya, "that your grandmother was wearing this on the day she died?"

"Yes. She'd asked me earlier in the week if she could borrow it to wear at Dr Marston's talk. She liked it so much that she asked to keep it for a while. It was her father's, so I couldn't exactly say no."

"And she wore it on a gold chain?"

"That's right."

"Thank you. That's all I needed, but I'm sure Dotty wants to hear more about the other pendants you mentioned." Keya sat back against the cushions on the sofa.

"Yes, I do," Dotty agreed, sitting up and addressing Beth.

"My great-grandfather was a lieutenant in the Second World War, and near the end, he was in charge of a small unit. He had the owl pendants made for all of its members."

"And was Pete Reynolds one of them?" Dotty asked.

"Yes!" Beth exclaimed. "Did you know Pete?"

"I didn't, but he sounded like a very interesting man. It seems you knew him well?"

"Yes. He'd been coming to the bookshop for several years. I think he even bought one of my great-grandad's books. I'd seen him around, but I didn't speak to him much. But then he overheard me talking to Gran about her dad and the trunk I found in the storeroom last autumn while organising old books for a school project."

"And that's when you discovered he knew your great-grandfather?"

"Yes. He said he hadn't known who we were when he first visited the bookshop, but he'd been drawn by all the references to owls. Over time, he must have picked up bits of conversation and then found my great-grandfather's name in some of the second-hand books."

"Did any of you talk to him about your great-grandfather or the war before you found the trunk?" Dotty asked.

Beth looked at her mother, who shrugged uncertainly.

"Gran might have, but she didn't say anything to me. Back then, it wasn't something I was interested in. Not until I opened the trunk and found his uniform, his medal, and that medallion with the swastika on it. Are those rare?"

Caught off guard, Dotty blinked before replying, "I've no idea. I'd need to see them first and probably consult an expert."

Beth started to stand, but Dotty quickly said, "I'm actually here to talk to you about Pete."

"Why?" Beth asked, her brow furrowing as she sat down again.

"The company I work for has been tasked by his nephew to clear his house and sell anything of value at auction. I'm afraid there isn't much."

"As I thought," Laura reflected. "He wasn't a wealthy man."

"Not in monetary terms," agreed Dotty, "but he also had an owl pendant, presumably the one your great grandfather gave him. And that is worth a bit."

"He'd never have sold it," Beth protested.

"I know," Dotty said gently. "And it wasn't the only valuable item he owned. Did he ever mention a painting?"

"A painting? No. Why? Should he have?"

"Because he left it, along with the owl pendant, to you," Dotty said.

Both Laura and Beth stared at her.

Then Laura asked, "You mean in his will?"

"In a letter, actually, which still needs to be verified by a lawyer. But as it's signed, dated, and witnessed, it appears legally binding. Did Pete ever tell you about this?"

"No. But then it wasn't as if he was ill," Beth protested. "The last time I saw him at the bookshop, he was so excited about the Christmas veterans' gathering. He said he'd finally be meeting up with an old friend he hadn't seen for years. I hope they did meet before he had his fall."

"His fall?" Keya queried.

Laura answered, "We heard about it later. He fell down some stairs and was taken to hospital. He never recovered and died in the New Year. So, no, we didn't know about the letter or the painting. I guess the owl pendant is valuable. It's gold, isn't it?"

"Yes, but the painting is likely to be the most valuable item. We've commissioned Dr Marston to research its history, especially since it's so unusual. We haven't found any record of it, and I'm curious about its origin." Dotty explained.

"How do you think Pete got hold of it? Was it a family treasure?" Beth asked, sounding surprised and a little anxious. Then her eyes widened as she added, "You don't think he stole it, do you?"

"We're not sure how he came to have it. It's by a lesser-known, but increasingly popular, Austrian artist. I'm afraid there will be a cost for the research, which, as the new owner, you'll need to cover." Dotty looked sincerely at Beth.

"What kind of costs are we talking about?" asked Laura.

"An initial £1,000, but Dr Marston estimated the total could be £3,000 to £5,000."

"That's a lot," protested Laura. "How much is the painting worth?"

"As it stands, twenty to thirty thousand pounds. But with provenance, it could be worth more."

"Goodness. But what if it didn't rightfully belong to Pete? Will Beth have to give it back?"

Not wanting to be drawn down that path, Dotty suggested, "Why don't we wait for Dr Marston's initial findings before we decide whether to continue his research?"

"That sounds sensible," Laura agreed.

“Can I see the painting?” Beth asked.

“Of course. It’s at the auction house, but I have a photo.” Dotty found the image on her phone and handed it to Beth.

“Oh,” Beth said, staring at the screen and sounding disappointed. “It’s not the sort of picture I would have expected Pete to own.”

“You mean because it’s a landscape rather than a military scene?”

“Yes, and it doesn’t look like England.”

“No, I think it’s Austria.”

As Beth handed Dotty’s phone back to her, she said, “I really appreciate Pete leaving it to me, but I’m not sure I want it hanging on my wall. It’s not like the owl pendant. That, I’d like to keep.”

“Why don’t we wait and see what Dr Marston finds out about the painting,” Laura suggested, echoing Dotty’s words, “before deciding anything.”

“We’ll also need confirmation from the lawyers that the letter and bequest are valid,” Dotty added.

"And the nephew might cause trouble," Keya pointed out.

"Pete told me he never visited and that we were like family to him," Beth said, sounding sad.

"That, I can believe." Keya rose to her feet.

As she did, Imogen Henshaw entered the room and asked, "You're with the police, aren't you?"

"Sort of," replied Keya. "Why?"

"I think I've found something on the computer you should see."

CHAPTER TWENTY-ONE

KEYA

Keya stood in a small home office space in Laura and Beth Fletcher's house, at the rear of The Owl's Nook, looking over Imogen Henshaw's shoulder.

Imogen was seated at a desk with an open laptop in front of her.

"What am I looking at?" asked Keya.

"These are some of the deleted files I found on the bookshop's system. I don't know if they're relevant to your investigation, but that young officer asked me to let you know if I found anything odd."

Keya presumed Warren was the officer Imogen was referring to, and that "you" was a generic term for the police.

She stared at the screen, which displayed three columns. The first appeared to be shorthand or a code of sorts, the second a list of addresses, and the third, prices.

"Have you asked Laura about them?" Keya enquired.

"She wasn't involved in the bookshop accounts." Imogen lowered her voice. "But Nicole acted strangely when I mentioned these files. I don't think she wanted me to find them."

Keya had to admit she'd had the same impression from the snippets of conversation she'd overheard between Imogen and Nicole.

"I'm still not sure what it all means, but first let me check where my colleague is," Keya said.

"I'll print you off a copy," Imogen suggested.

"Two, please," Keya replied, holding her phone to her ear.

"I'm just pulling up to the bookshop now," Warren said distractedly when he answered.

"I'm in the house," Keya replied before ending the conversation.

Returning her focus to the screen, Keya asked, "What do you think the entries in the first column mean?"

"The top line looks like shorthand for something, and the letters underneath might be product or order codes. They could just be books, but…"

"But what?" Keya prompted.

"All the other orders I've seen include the title and author's name. I'm not sure why these are different."

The doorbell rang, and Keya left the office to answer it. As she expected, Warren stood waiting. He raised his eyebrows enquiringly at her.

"Come and look at this," she said.

She led him back to the office, where he stared at the computer screen as Imogen handed them each a set of printed sheets.

"What does it mean?" Warren asked.

"We don't know, but…" Keya hesitated, considering her next move. "I think we should ask Nicole."

Warren turned to her, a questioning look in his eyes. "OK. Where is she?"

"Sorting out book orders," Keya remembered.

"I'll fetch her," Imogen offered, failing to hide a note of satisfaction.

Keya returned to the sitting room, where Laura and Dotty were still chatting. Beth was nowhere to be seen.

"Do you recognise this?" Keya asked Laura, handing her the top sheet of the printout.

After glancing at it, Laura replied, "It looks like bookshop orders. I haven't been involved with that side of the business, but I guess I'll have to learn how to manage it now. What do these letters mean? They don't look like book titles."

"That's what we're wondering," Keya admitted.

"May I?" Dotty asked.

Laura passed her the sheet, and Dotty was still studying it when Nicole entered the room. Her earlier petulance was gone, but her eyes narrowed as she glanced from Keya to Warren, and her jaw tightened.

"Please sit down," Keya said, gesturing to the chair where Beth had been sitting earlier. Warren remained by the door, notebook and pen in hand, while Keya sat on the sofa next to Dotty.

"I couldn't help overhearing your reluctance for Imogen to recover some deleted files earlier," Keya began. "Why was that?"

"As I said," Nicole replied defensively, "we're trying to create a new system, not patch up the old one." She glared at Imogen, who appeared in the doorway.

"So it wasn't because you didn't want her to find this?" Keya asked, taking the printed sheet from Dotty and handing it to Nicole.

Nicole's eyes widened in recognition as she bit her lip.

"These aren't ordinary book orders, are they? There are no titles or authors. So, what are they?" pressed Keya.

"I don't know," stammered Nicole.

"I think you do," remarked Keya in a steady, firm voice. "And from what I can tell, only you and Helen had access to the system. Did you delete these files?"

The question was a gamble, but Keya knew she'd struck a nerve when Nicole gasped, and a flush spread across her cheeks.

"Come on, Nicole. It's obvious you know about these orders. That's what they are, aren't they? And you tried to cover them up. Why? Was it something illegal Helen was involved in?"

Nicole's eyes bulged.

That shocked her, Keya thought. So, not illegal, or not involving Helen?

Dotty stepped in. "It's a lovely place, the bookshop, but a bit quiet for a young woman like you. I bet you have some great ideas for modernising the shop."

"Oh, yes," Nicole said, smiling briefly at Dotty. Then her face fell.

"But Helen wasn't interested. She wanted to run it the way she always had, until she met Imogen at that veterans' charity event before Christmas.

After that, she came back with all these ideas about taking the business forward. Most of them were things I'd already suggested, but I'm not some young whizz kid from a posh family whose face is splashed all over social media. I'm just a bookshop assistant."

Nicole refused to look at Imogen, slumping back in her chair instead.

Keya gave Dotty an approving glance. Dotty had managed to get Nicole talking, and they'd confirmed the link between Helen, the bookshop, and Imogen. Was the veterans' event the same one where Pete Reynolds had taken a tumble?

Returning to Nicole and the files, Keya softened her tone as she asked, "Was this a sideline?"

Nicole folded her arms and clamped her lips together.

"We just need to make sure it's not connected to Helen's death," Dotty said reasonably.

"It isn't," Nicole snapped, her voice rising. "And if it's Helen's death you want to know about, you should ask her brother."

Nicole's eyes flicked to Imogen, her expression hardening, before she pointed a finger at her.

"Seb? What does he have to do with this?" Imogen asked, startled.

"I don't know," Nicole replied. "But I saw him get out of his car and walk towards the bookshop entrance as I was driving off with my deliveries."

Imogen sounded puzzled as she stated, "But I've never even seen Seb with a book. What would he be doing here?"

CHAPTER TWENTY-TWO

DOTTY

Dotty turned the pages of the new auction catalogue. It was mid-morning on Friday, and several boxes of brochures had just been delivered to Akemans.

One of the relocated stallholders had already complained about them, so she and Clara had moved the boxes into their new office space at the back of the auction house.

Clara sat at her desk, which faced the entrance and doubled as the reception area, flipping through another catalogue.

"Um," she said, sounding confused.

Dotty looked up. "Have you found something?"

"Can you check page eight?"

Dotty turned to the page and saw an image of a Tiffany grandfather tall-case clock. But as she looked closer, her stomach sank. "Oh no, the lot numbers are all wrong!"

"That's what I thought," Clara nodded. "What should we do about them? I could change a few by hand, but all of them?" She gestured toward the stack of unopened boxes, all containing brochures.

"You'd never get through them," Dotty said, glancing forlornly at the boxes. "And some catalogues have already been delivered to Amanda and picked up by the delivery company"

She sat back, considering the problem. The descriptions of the items and their estimated values were correct, and it was only the lot numbers which were wrong. How much did that matter now? As long as they were correct for auction day…

She made her decision just as Zach entered the room.

"Let's leave the brochures as they are, since we need to distribute them. But can you create a new page or two with the correct lot numbers? Then we can ask the printers to make copies to insert into the remaining catalogues and hand out as amendments during the viewings for anyone who's already picked one up."

"Oh, that's a good idea. Do you want images on the sheet too?" Clara asked.

"No, just the descriptions. Thank you."

Dotty looked up as Zach approached her desk.

"Problem?" he enquired.

"When isn't there?" Dotty replied with a resigned smile. "But I think we've got it sorted, haven't we, Clara?"

"Yes. An insert for auction day and the viewings will work," Clara confirmed, returning to her computer.

"It's just frustrating when things aren't done properly. But perhaps it was our fault, not the printers'," Dotty considered.

Clara looked up and gave her a pointed look that clearly said she blamed the printers.

Zach, who was carrying a grey rucksack, said, "I have a meeting later with Marmaduke, Gilly, and Aunt Beanie. Would you like to join us?"

"Now the catalogues are as sorted as they can be, my main work for the week is done, so sure. But can I know what you're proposing before the meeting, or is it a secret?"

"No, I'd love to run through it with you. I just haven't asked earlier because you've been out of the office."

"Yes, I was at The Owl's Nook yesterday," Dotty said, before telling him all about Pete's letter, Beth, the painting, and the owl pendant. As she finished, her phone rang.

"Sorry, I need to take this," she said.

"No problem. I need to catch up with the stallholders in the front office and check that everyone who needs power has it. Then I'll be in the cafe if you want to join me."

Dotty smiled at him as she answered her call.

"Good morning, Dotty. This is Hugo Marston."

"Dr Marston." She hadn't expected to hear from him so soon.

"Please, call me Hugo. I've made some progress, and your painting is quite fascinating. I'm coming to Akemans for a meeting at the cafe and wondered if you'd like to catch up quickly."

"Certainly. I'm also heading to the café. When do you expect to be there?"

"Half an hour, perhaps sooner," replied Hugo.

After answering a few emails, Dotty stood up, looked at Clara, and asked, "Do you have enough work to be getting on with?"

"Oh, yes. After I've finished formatting the insert, I need to answer some emails. Why is it that people always ask when the next auction is or what time viewings start when the information is clearly on our website?"

"That's just how people are. It's easier to fire off an email than take the time to look it up for themselves," Dotty replied, smiling empathetically at Clara before leaving the office.

The main auction room was starting to come alive. Dotty smiled. How much nicer it was for the space to be used rather than sitting empty. But they couldn't move people in and out every month. They needed space for the auctions. If they were to continue.

She nodded, acknowledging a man selling a collection of farm equipment, including old metal milk churns, a hand plough, and metal buckets in various states of disrepair.

The range of items sold by the individual stallholders always fascinated her.

There were, of course, sellers of pottery, jewellery, and antique silverware, but also those with collections of old stamps, cameras, or her favourite, vintage clothing. But she couldn't stop and look now. Zach was waiting for her.

Moving into the antique centre, she passed several stalls and the area still cordoned off with yellow tape. More plaster dust lay in pale patches on the stone floor.

The cafe was busy with animated conversations, and she caught the smell of fresh coffee and frying bacon as she entered.

Her stomach rumbled as she reached Zach's table and noticed the partially eaten bacon sandwich beside the book he was reading. She'd expected him to be poring over papers. "What's that?" she asked.

"Checkpoint Charlie: *The Cold War, the Berlin Wall, and the Most Dangerous Place on Earth* by Iain MacGregor," Zach said, flipping over the cover to read the full title. "I picked it up from The Owl's Nook. It makes a pleasant change from reading about the Second World War, although the two are, of course, linked."

"You mean the Cold War was a consequence of the actual war?"

"Yes. And can you imagine? Countries that thought they were free, and people who survived the war, found themselves part of another oppressive regime. Germany was split in half, with families separated, neighbours turning against each other, and entire communities living in fear. There are some incredible stories in this book."

As Aunt Beanie approached, wearing a headscarf of yellows and purples, Dotty added, "And then the wall fell. I learned about that in my school history lessons."

"Oh, the Berlin Wall," Aunt Beanie said, glancing at Zach's book. "I remember watching it on the news all evening. The reporters couldn't keep up. The crowds, the shouting, people climbing the wall. It was extraordinary. And monumental. It was symbolic, you see, of the Russian hold on Eastern Europe. And then, just days later, the Velvet Revolution in Czechoslovakia. Everything seemed to be changing overnight. It makes you wonder about all the people who lived through it, doesn't it? What they suffered, and what happened to all those who made them suffer."

"What do you mean?" Dotty asked.

Zach tapped his book and answered, "In East Germany, there was an authority called the Stasi. They even recruited children to spy on their own families, controlling people through fear and betrayal. And when the regime fell, many of them just disappeared, taking their secrets with them."

"Precisely," Aunt Beanie agreed. "We spent all our time wondering what happened to the Nazis, prosecuting them for their crimes, but what about all those who escaped East Germany and the Soviet bloc. Who knows? They may even be living amongst us now."

"I doubt it," Zach responded. "Or if they are, they'll be old men and women."

Thinking of old men and women, Dotty noticed Matthew Henshaw being guided to a table by Zivah. Although he moved slowly, leaning heavily on his walking stick, he carried a quiet strength and an air of calm resolve that reflected a life well lived.

By his side was the ever-vigilant Radek, whose eyes darted from Matthew to customers in the room. When he caught Dotty's eye, she smiled, but he ignored her, continuing his surveillance.

"I'm not sure how much I like that Radek," commented Aunt Beanie. "Although you can't fault his dedication to protecting Matthew."

At that moment, the group passed a table, and a man jumped up abruptly, reaching into his jacket pocket.

Radek immediately stiffened as the man stepped towards them.

Gasping, Dotty watched as Radek seemed to act instinctively, grabbing the man's arm and twisting it behind his back.

There was a howl of pain, and the man cried, "What are you doing?"

"That was quick," Zach remarked. "I wonder where he learned to react like that."

"I told you I wasn't sure about Radek," Aunt Beanie said. "He's not what he seems."

"Are any of us?" Dotty considered as Matthew reached out, placing his hand on Radek's shoulder. As he murmured something, Radek's posture eased, and he released his grip.

The man rubbed his arm and blustered, "What was the meaning of that? I should report you to the police."

"I am the police," said Keya, joining the group.

"You…" The man looked at her in confusion.

Keya explained. "I switch roles between my police work and running the cafe." She offered the man a reassuring smile.

"Yes, well, it was you I wanted to speak to. I'm a rep with a soft drinks company."

"Then why don't we sit down?" Keya suggested, nodding subtly at Zivah, who led Matthew and Radek to an empty table.

CHAPTER TWENTY-THREE

DOTTY

The customers in the Waterwheel Cafe settled down after the commotion caused by Radek Novák confronting a rep from a soft drinks firm.

"We're meeting later, aren't we?" Aunt Beanie asked Zach, who was finishing the last bite of his bacon sandwich.

Dotty sat down next to him as he replied, "Yes, and Marmaduke is coming, isn't he?"

"After the way Gilly's been harassing him this week over closing a section of the antique centre, definitely. And if not, I'll drive over and collect him myself."

She glanced behind her and added, "Now, I need to speak to Norman." Turning, she walked towards the drinks counter where Norman was working.

Zach pushed his book aside and pulled a folder from his grey rucksack. This was exactly what Dotty had been expecting.

An organised and well-thought-out proposal to present to Marmaduke, addressing the wall repairs between the auction house and antique centre, as well as the issues with the first floor.

But as Zach unfurled several A3 sheets with detailed drawings, Dotty leaned forward, intrigued. These looked far more complicated than a simple wall repair.

"What's this?" she asked.

"Just give me a minute," Zach replied. Once his papers were neatly arranged, he placed his hands on the table and said, "The problem with the old mill wall, which is affecting the first floor and causing the falling plaster, is actually a fantastic opportunity."

"It is?" Dotty asked, surprised.

"Yes. After seeing the transformation of the auction room with all the stalls, bustle, and people, I'm more convinced than ever about the ideas I've been working on after visiting other auction houses…"

"When have you done that?" Dotty asked, puzzled. Zach hadn't said anything to her about his research.

"What do you think I've been doing for the past couple of months? Sitting at home by myself?"

That was exactly what she'd thought. Although she knew he'd been visiting historic houses and training for an upcoming seven-kilometre run at Blenheim Palace.

Zach smiled indulgently. "I didn't bother you because I know you've been busy here sorting out all the issues and managing the extra country house sale at Marchwood Hall earlier this month."

"I like visiting other auction houses," Dotty mused aloud.

"Great, because I'd love you to see a few, and judge how my ideas might work in practice."

"What ideas?" Dotty asked.

Zach slid the pile of A3 sheets across the table, so they were positioned between them. “For redesigning and upgrading the auction house,” he said.

“Oh, I thought we were only doing repairs,” Dotty replied, staring at the drawing in front of her.

“Why stop there? If we want the auction house to succeed, we need to modernise it, like many of the ones I’ve visited. The current auction room is underutilised, and finding a permanent use for it will help fund my proposal.”

Dotty sat back, her eyes on Zach. “I agree it’s a shame for the auction room to sit empty outside sale times. It looks great now with the all the stalls, but how do we juggle the monthly auctions with another use?”

“By moving the auctions upstairs and using the storerooms for viewings,” Zach explained. “Or we could convert the storerooms for another purpose and keep everything for the sales in the main auction room, but in a more organised way. I’m not sure of the exact logistics yet, but first we need to create the extra space and a purpose-built auction room.”

“OK,” Dotty said dubiously, just managing to keep up. “And where is that going to be?”

“On the underutilised first floor,” Zach declared.

“Of the antique centre?” Dotty queried.

“Yes, and also a mezzanine floor over part of the auction house. Look here.” Zach placed his finger on the plan, guiding her to the area he was describing.

“This is empty space in the main auction room, and this is the first floor of the antique centre. By creating a modern, purpose-built space for hosting auctions, we can arrange rows of conference-style seating and install proper lighting that supports the online platform. It’ll be clear, crisp, and professional.”

Zach looked proudly at Dotty before continuing, “We can still display the best pictures and objects around the perimeter of the room, but the main area will be dedicated to seating. I know Akemans used to hold valuation days in the past, and this space, which we can insulate and heat, would be perfect for that.”

Dotty certainly liked the idea of a dedicated auction room with a modern, professional feel. And one that was heated. That would be a bonus.

But she had her reservations as she asked, “How do we do all this? And what will it cost?”

“Let’s set the expenditure aside for now. I’ve been working on these plans for a while, so I actually had a structural engineer assess the buildings. That’s why I’ve been so concerned about the first floor and the falling plaster. It really isn’t safe.”

Zach gave Dotty a reassuring smile before continuing, “The party wall between the buildings is the issue. Over time, it’s settled unevenly, with the added strain of supporting two different structures. Add to this the vibration of traffic on the road, and the result is structural instability requiring reinforcement, cracks that need repairing, areas where bricks must be replaced, and mortar that needs repointing.”

“Oh dear. That doesn’t sound good.”

“It’ll be fine as long as the repairs are done properly, and soon. The wall needs reinforcing with steel beams and possibly some underpinning to support the existing foundations. It’s not a cheap job, but since it has to be done anyway, it's the perfect opportunity to include additional works and create an opening between the two buildings. More steelwork will be needed, but tackling everything together will be more economical in the long run. Other necessary repairs include replacing damaged bricks and reinforcing the first floor to support the extra weight of the auction room."

"It sounds interesting," Dotty said hesitantly, "but also really expensive. I don't see how Marmaduke will agree to it."

"He has to do something. If he leaves the wall much longer without undertaking any repairs, we could be forced to close the entire antique centre. And with it, the cafe and the auction house."

"Is it really that serious?" But she hardly needed to ask. The intensity in Zach's eyes and the tight line of his mouth told her it was.

Dotty looked round the buzzing cafe. Dr Marston—Hugo—had joined Matthew and Radek, and was talking earnestly to them. Seb had also arrived and joined the discussion. Dotty wondered if Lynn or Warren had spoken to him yet, and whether they'd discovered why he had been at The Owl's Nook on Saturday afternoon.

And what about the cafe?

"We can't close the cafe," she insisted, focusing back on Zach. "Not after all the work Keya has put in. It really is the heart of Akemans now. Not that I don't think we can revive the auction house, and I know Gilly can bring the antique centre back to life, especially in summer with all the tourists and coach tours. But the money?"

Zach cleared his throat, and Dotty looked at him enquiringly.

"I wanted to discuss that with you."

"Me? I don't have the kind of money needed for this project," she protested.

"But I do," Zach said seriously. "I've run some figures on different ways to utilise the auction house space, such as for events, parties or conferences, or converting the storerooms into offices or co-working spaces, and I'm confident I can achieve a return on my investment. But…"

Dotty raised her eyebrows, waiting to hear the catch.

"I'll need to be in charge, so I can make sure the right financial decisions are made, even if not everyone agrees. And…" This time he looked fondly at Dotty. "It depends on whether you want me to stick around."

"Oh, I do," Dotty said without thinking.

"But as a friend, or something more?" Zach pressed.

Dotty held Zach's gaze. His intense hazel eyes were full of quiet determination, softened by a flicker of vulnerability. She noticed the way his mouth curved slightly, as if offering her reassurance without words, and the stillness of his usually energetic demeanour.

Her chest tightened, caught between the warmth of his presence and the weight of everything else she was juggling. She didn't want him to leave, but taking the next step felt like uncharted territory.

"Zach…" she began, her voice soft, uncertain, the unspoken words hanging in the air between them. She let out a breath she hadn't realised she was holding and fidgeted with the edge of the paper in front of her. "You've been such a reassuring presence. I've really enjoyed the time we've spent together this past year."

Zach's lips lifted in a tentative smile, but his eyes stayed locked on hers.

"I am not planning on going anywhere for the moment, Dotty. But when I moved to Burford, I said I would give you six months to consider what you wanted, and the clock is ticking. If I am going to invest in Akemans, in you, in us, then I need to know you are in it too, if that is what you want."

Dotty looked down at her hands, gathering her thoughts. Finally, she met his gaze again. "I want the auction house to succeed. For Akemans to be successful, for Gilly and Keya. And you've been such a help already."

He took hold of her hand, his voice warm. "And what about you? About us?"

Dotty hesitated, feeling the heat rise in her cheeks. Then she gave him a small smile. "I can't promise anything more than that today… but I do know I don't want to lose you."

Zach's shoulders relaxed, and he nodded, the smile on his face now reaching his eyes. "That's enough for the moment. For these proposals. But remember, I don't want to pressure you, but I can't hang around forever if you're not committed to being with me for the long term."

Dotty felt a flutter of panic. Would she be able to cope without him? Then she took a deep breath. Of course she could. Just as she had after her husband Al died. And even if she and Zach deepened their relationship, it was imperative she stood on her own two feet. She had to retain her independence.

She heard a cough, and Aunt Beanie said in a dry tone, "When you two lovebirds have finished, we have a meeting to attend."

CHAPTER TWENTY-FOUR

DOTTY

As Zach tidied away his papers in preparation for the meeting about Akemans and his proposals to repair and modernise it, Dr Hugo Marston approached the table where Dotty was still sitting in the Waterwheel Cafe.

Behind him, she noticed Matthew Henshaw raising and lowering his hands in a calming gesture as he spoke to his grandson, Seb.

“Is now a good time to discuss your Josef Stoitzner painting?” Hugo asked.

Dotty glanced at Zach, who was placing his folder back into his rucksack.

"What do you think?" she asked.

"I'm happy to start the meeting and outline the plans I've already discussed with you. But I think it will be useful for you to join the discussion in, say," he checked his watch, "ten, perhaps fifteen minutes."

"That should give us enough time," Hugo agreed. "What I have to say won't take long, although I would like to see the picture itself first."

"Of course," Dotty said, standing up. "It's in the office."

As she turned to leave, Zach added, "We'll be upstairs in Gilly's office."

Walking through the antique centre, Hugo remarked on various items displayed on the stalls. "It's an interesting collection. I must set aside a few hours one day to have a proper look around. Oh, and you have more stalls through here," he said as they entered the old auction reception.

The door between the two buildings was propped open, and a blackboard displaying a handwritten message inviting visitors to explore the additional stalls next door stood beside it.

"This is just a temporary measure while we undertake some repairs. But it means we've had to move the auction office," Dotty explained as she led him through the main auction room to the rear office.

Marion was standing behind Clara, and they were both staring intently at a computer screen, when Dotty and Hugo entered.

"Hello, Marion. It's been a long time," Hugo said.

Marion straightened, turned, and smiled cordially at him. "Yes, it has. One could almost say a lifetime."

"It's good to see you back here."

Marion had been working at Akemans when Dotty first started, but they had both spent time away before returning to their current roles.

"Thank you. Are you here about the painting?" Marion asked as Dotty collected it from a rack Zach had installed.

"Oh yes!" Clara exclaimed. "What have you discovered?"

"I'd like to examine it first," Hugo said as Dotty handed him the picture.

He murmured phrases like, "incredible use of light," "classic Secessionist technique," and "remarkable detail in the foreground."

Finally, he looked up thoughtfully and confirmed, "It is undoubtedly a Josef Stoitzner, painted in the early twentieth century. His work is known for blending traditional landscapes with subtle Secessionist influences. A fine piece, though not one of his most famous."

"Do we know who originally owned it?" Clara asked eagerly, clearly hoping her research had been on the right track.

"I'm still investigating that angle, although I have found records showing that a Herr Friedrich Albrecht, a wealthy industrialist from Saxony, purchased this painting along with two others in the early 1930s. They were displayed at his estate near Leipzig until the beginning of the Second World War. He paid 500 Reichsmarks for this one and 1,500 in total."

"Oh wow," Clara said. "Was that a lot of money back then?"

"For the 1930s? Quite a sum, although not extravagant for someone like Herr Albrecht. He was a collector with an eye for both traditional and modern art. A man of refined tastes. Unfortunately, many of his more valuable pieces were seized by the Nazis during the war, just as they looted countless private collections."

"And this painting?" Clara asked, her eyes bright with excitement.

"This one?" Hugo tapped the edge of the frame thoughtfully. "There are no records of it after 1945, which isn't uncommon for works like this. But I'll admit, it's not the kind of piece the Nazis would have prioritised. They tended to focus on more prestigious or well-known artists."

"How do you think it ended up in Pete Reynolds' hands?" Dotty asked, her brow furrowing. "He didn't have anything else like it. Nothing much of value at all, apart from a gold owl pendant."

"A gold owl pendant? Not the one Helen Fletcher—God rest her soul—was wearing at my talk?"

"A similar one. We think Helen's father and Pete were in the same unit at the end of the war. They called themselves The Little Owls after an interpreter who was with them and had sharp instincts that kept them out of trouble."

"Now that is interesting," Hugo said as he handed the painting back to Dotty. "Do you mind if I undertake some more research?"

Dotty hesitated.

"If it's the cost you're concerned about, we can sort that out later. To be honest, now that I've started this case, I know I won't be able to stop until I understand exactly how and why this painting," he glanced at it, "ended up here."

"Thank you," Dotty said, relieved. "The ownership of the painting isn't entirely clear yet. It looks like Pete Reynolds left it to Helen Fletcher's granddaughter, but I'm still waiting for the lawyers to confirm whether his letter is legally binding."

"Another layer of intrigue. This only gets better," Dr Hugo commented.

Although his voice retained a professional tone, his eyes sparkled much like Clara's had done earlier. Dotty realised that researching the history of the painting was clearly as compelling to him as investigating an unexplained death was to her.

"And now I must return to Matthew Henshaw and his party."

"Do they also have paintings with mysterious pasts?" Clara asked.

"Do you know, I'm not sure. I've been told that Matthew has a small but valuable collection of art and antiques, although I haven't seen it myself."

Hugo paused, straightened and adjusted his glasses. With an air of satisfaction and a note of pride in his voice, he added, "After my talk, Matthew mentioned he was planning to leave money to several charities, including the institution I represent. He's passionate about supporting the recovery and preservation of artefacts lost during times of conflict. And the sums involved could be quite significant."

"I shouldn't think his grandchildren are happy about that," Marion remarked.

Hugo hesitated, then said with a faintly apologetic smile, "I probably shouldn't say too much, but let's just say Sebastian isn't thrilled. There's been talk of Imogen, who's doing rather well for herself, helping to oversee the distribution of funds to ensure they're used appropriately. Understandably, that hasn't gone down terribly well with her brother. That's actually why I stepped away. To give them some privacy to talk things through."

"What about Radek?" Dotty asked, recalling the earlier incident in the cafe.

"I don't believe he has much say over the donations, but he's still taking a precautionary stance. He's even suggested that Matthew's name not be linked to the donations. Personally, I think it might be better if his company, Athena Trading, acts as the benefactor. But, not surprisingly, Sebastian disagrees."

Dotty and Hugo continued discussing the challenges of tracking down artwork and valuables lost during wars as they walked back through the antique centre to the Waterwheel Cafe. When they reached Matthew Henshaw's table, Dotty said goodbye to Hugo and started to move away.

But Matthew called out, "Miss Sayers."

She didn't like to correct him and explain that, as a widow, she was actually Mrs Sayers. Instead, she smiled and said, "Please, call me Dotty."

"Dotty, we haven't met, but I saw you at Dr Marston's talk, and I understand you've taken over running the auction house."

"Yes, that's correct," Dotty replied simply.

"I've bought and sold a few items over the years at Akemans. They've always acted very professionally. I'm sure you can weather the current storm. Businesses are like life. They go through phases. I started as a young man with nothing, and now I have enough to contribute to worthwhile causes. It takes resilience to keep going. Sometimes we have to fight for what matters, like my friend Radek, who understands that better than most."

Radek jerked his head up, momentarily caught off guard. Unlike the man earlier, he clearly didn't consider Dotty or Hugo a threat.

"He had to fight for his freedom, didn't you?"

"Er, yes, sir. It was a struggle, but 9th November 1989. That changed everything."

Matthew blinked, then turned back to Dotty. “But I’m sure you can find a way to make sure your business survives. And even thrives.”

Dotty wasn’t sure how he knew so much about Akemans, but she wasn’t entirely surprised. And it seemed as though Zach was the one finding the solution, not her, and for that, she felt both grateful and proud.

“I mustn’t keep you,” Matthew said, but then added, “I may have an item or two to send your way in the near future.”

Dotty smiled politely, then turned as Hugo sat down.

It was time to join Zach and see how his discussions about Akemans’ future were progressing.

CHAPTER TWENTY-FIVE

DOTTY

"We can't possibly afford this," Marmaduke declared as Dotty entered Gilly's office on the first floor above the antique centre.

Marmaduke was sitting in Gilly's office chair behind her desk, while Aunt Beanie, Zach, and Gilly were seated on upright wooden chairs arranged in a semi-circle in front of him. Dotty removed a pile of papers from another chair, lifted it, and placed it next to Gilly's before sitting down.

"Marmaduke, don't be so stubborn," argued Aunt Beanie. "Don't you see that we have to make some kind of investment? Have you looked downstairs? Red and white cones and yellow tape. It resembles a crime scene more than an antique centre. And even if we wanted to, we can't hold any more auctions until we've moved the stalls out of the auction house."

"But…" Marmaduke blustered.

"How much are we talking?" Gilly asked Zach, her tone laced with worry.

"I've been told somewhere in the region of £100,000 to £150,000, but I won't lie to you, the costs could easily rise to £200,000 if the repairs are more extensive," Zach admitted.

"Oh dear," muttered Gilly. "We'd need to take out a loan to cover that cost."

"I haven't been in debt for the past thirty years," protested Marmaduke, "and I'm not about to start now!"

"Brother dear, I think that sums it up. I've been telling you for a while that it's time to pass the business on. Besides, with your shooting in the winter and golfing in the summer, how much time do you really have to spend at Akemans?" Aunt Beanie countered.

"I'm at the estate agency most days," Marmaduke claimed.

"Which raises an excellent point," Aunt Beanie continued. "While it was a good idea to have that branch of the company support the auction house in the beginning, I don't think the two businesses are that closely connected anymore."

"Not after all the newspaper allegations," agreed Gilly.

"Are you suggesting, Bernadette," Zach said, using Aunt Beanie's full name, "that we separate the estate agency business from the antiques side, leaving Marmaduke to oversee the former?"

"That is an excellent proposal, Zach," Aunt Beanie said, fixing her brother with a firm stare.

"But…" Marmaduke protested again.

Dotty wondered if Zach and Aunt Beanie had discussed their approach beforehand and planned to back Marmaduke into a corner.

“Who will run the rest of Akemans?” Marmaduke narrowed his eyes and pressed his lips together as he stared at Gilly.

“Er,” Gilly muttered, her forehead creasing with uncertainty.

“Zach,” stated Aunt Beanie firmly. “I’ve said before that he’s the perfect man for the role. Not that a woman couldn’t manage the job, but Gilly and Dotty have their hands full…”

“Not me,” Dotty said quickly, her voice tinged with alarm.

“There we go,” Aunt Beanie confirmed with a decisive nod. “And Zach has run his own business before, and it was clearly successful since he sold it for a considerable sum.”

Dotty knew Zach had run a company related to computers or technology, and that he’d built it up and sold it well, but she didn’t know the details or how much he’d made. She wondered just what meetings he and Aunt Beanie had held together.

“Zach?” Marmaduke cried, sounding incredulous. “But he’s not family.”

“Precisely,” pronounced Aunt Beanie, her tone edged with irony.

Gilly pushed back the ringlets of orange hair that had fallen in front of her face. Looking anxiously between Aunt Beanie and Zach, she then turned to her father and, in a tentative tone, said, “I agree with Aunt Beanie. I think we need to bring someone in who’s not family. Besides, we’ve already appointed Dotty to a managerial role, and she’s not a relative.”

Marmaduke gave Dotty a fleeting look that made her feel as though she didn’t count.

“But I’m still worried about the cost and the time it’ll take to complete these works,” Gilly said quietly, a frown creasing her forehead.

“The works are bound to cause disruption,” Zach acknowledged. “And some stallholders will leave to find alternative spaces, but that’s why I think we should do it now. Get the worst over with, and then rebuild the business. Maybe this is also an opportunity to upgrade the antique centre too, not just the auction house.”

“More money,” muttered Marmaduke.

"But an excellent suggestion. What do you have in mind?" asked Aunt Beanie.

"I'm not sure," Zach admitted, glancing at Gilly.

"Upgrading the lighting would be fantastic," Gilly began, warming to the idea. "And providing each stall with its own electrical point. Then there's the plastering and painting for the walls and ceiling, and…"

"Stop," declared Marmaduke. "This is getting out of hand. We're not restarting the whole business."

Dotty remembered Matthew's words about phases of business and needing resilience and, after a moment of hesitation, she summoned all her resolve to say, "Maybe that's exactly what we do need to do. Begin again. Reinvent ourselves. Move forward with fresh ideas and purpose."

The others fell silent, staring at her. Had she spoken out of turn?

"Bravo," Aunt Beanie proclaimed, clapping her hands.

Marmaduke appeared speechless.

"I don't disagree," Gilly said cautiously, "but the cost…"

Aunt Beanie turned to Zach.

"I suppose you have a solution for that too," Marmaduke said drily.

Aunt Beanie nodded decisively.

Zach took a deep breath and said, "I do have an investor."

"Who?" Gilly enquired.

"Me."

Marmaduke laughed, but the sound died in his throat under Aunt Beanie's withering stare.

"You want to take over my business AND invest in it?" Marmaduke asked, incredulous.

"If I can't back myself and my decisions, how can I expect any of you to do so?" Zach replied, looking at each of them in turn.

"And he's only repeating what we did when we set up the business," Aunt Beanie added.

"That was different," Marmaduke said, pinching his lips together and crossing his arms.

“Not really, Dad,” Gilly replied in a placatory tone.

“What we all want,” Dotty ventured, hoping she wasn’t saying more than she should, “is for Akemans to keep going, and to flourish and be successful. And at the moment, that’s not going to happen. We’ve already lost two auctions this year, part of the antique centre is closed, stallholders are giving notice, and our reputation is in shreds.”

“I don’t think it’s that bad,” Marmaduke protested.

“Which part of what Dotty said isn’t true?” Gilly asked. “And she didn’t even mention the repairs we have to undertake just to keep the doors open.”

Everyone turned to Marmaduke.

Finally, he said, “It’s clear you’ve already made up your minds, all of you, but I can’t say I agree with your decision.”

“So can we minute that you’re formally handing over control of Akemans to Zach,” Aunt Beanie pressed, “and that you’ll form a separate company with the estate agency business?”

"I suppose I'll have to. You've not exactly given me a choice." Marmaduke stood and stalked out of Gilly's office.

"You could wish us luck!" Aunt Beanie called after him.

CHAPTER TWENTY-SIX

DOTTY

Dotty and Gilly left Zach and Aunt Beanie to continue discussing the plans to repair and modernise Akemans.

They descended the metal staircase to the ground floor of the antique centre, but Gilly paused halfway, her gaze sweeping across the stalls.

“We’ve done so much to build this up,” she said, her tone tinged with both pride and concern. “I know my dad sometimes seems indifferent, but without his vision, this business would never have got off the ground.”

“And Aunt Beanie?” Dotty prompted.

"Oh, I'm sure she was a great help, with plenty of input, but it was Dad who came up with the idea for the antique centre and paid for the works."

"Do you think that's why it's so difficult for him to hand over control to someone else?"

"Yes, especially, as he said, to someone who isn't family. It's also tough for him to admit there are problems that need fixing."

"As someone reminded me today, business, like life, goes through phases. And you had some fantastic ideas for improving the antique centre. Imagine how much better it could look with improved lighting, fresh paint, and maybe some plants and splashes of colour to brighten it up."

Dotty glanced around at the stalls, picturing the potential.

"You're right, changes like that could make a huge difference. I should write all this down and share it with Zach to see if he can include the ideas in his plan."

"I'm sure he'd be thrilled to combine your suggestions with his to create a modern, welcoming, and profitable space."

"And I think I'll speak to some of the stallholders too, and see if they have any thoughts about reviving the place."

With renewed energy, Gilly descended the remaining stairs and stepped onto the stone-flagged floor. She greeted a stall holder with a friendly wave before crossing over to speak to another.

Dotty watched her for a moment with an indulgent smile. She was just about to return to the auction house when she heard Lynn's voice, "Hello, Dotty."

Shaking her head to dispel thoughts of building improvements, Dotty turned her attention to Lynn, who was accompanied by Warren in his police constable's uniform.

"Do you have business in the antique centre?" she asked, her tone edged with concern.

"No, I'm meeting Keya for a Friday lunchtime catch-up to compare notes on the Stow-on-the-Wold case."

"The one at The Owl's Nook?"

“Yes, and Warren mentioned you were there with Keya yesterday.”

Dotty glanced at Warren, whose cheeks flushed faintly.

“I was on Akemans’ business, and I met Keya after she finished working on the crime scene.”

“What business?” Lynn asked, her tone curious rather than accusatory.

“We’ve been instructed to sell items from a house clearance at auction, but it turns out two of them have been bequeathed to Beth Fletcher.”

“That’s interesting,” remarked Lynn thoughtfully. Then, looking at Dotty, she added, “If you’re not too busy, would you like to join us for our meeting? I always value your perspective on a case, and you can tell me more about those items.”

They entered the cafe and met Keya, who was carrying a tray laden with bowls of soup. She gestured towards the rear of the room and said, “I’ve reserved that table in the corner for us. I’ll join you in a minute, but as you can see…” She motioned towards a group of three women dressed in country tweeds. "I'm a little tied up right now."

"The Friday lunchtime crowd," Lynn commented, leading the way to the table Keya had indicated.

"It's wonderful to see the cafe thriving," Dotty replied.

As she sat down opposite Lynn, with Warren between them, Lynn remarked in a thoughtful tone, "You say that as if other parts of the business aren't doing so well."

Dotty gave her a quick overview of the challenges facing the auction house and antique centre. It felt like a relief to confide in someone not directly involved with the business.

"That does sound tough," Lynn said sympathetically. "Dealing with building issues on top of the damage to your reputation must be really challenging."

"It is," Dotty agreed. "I don't think Gilly and I could sort it out on our own, which is why I really appreciate Zach's help. And not just his plans for the physical repairs but also his ideas for reinventing the entire business. They're actually really exciting." She shared Zach's proposals with Lynn and Warren.

When she'd finished, she took a deep breath and apologised, "Sorry, I didn't mean to burden you with our problems."

"Not at all. We all need someone to talk to, and your friends are mostly involved in the business. That's why I enjoy discussing cases with you. You're not part of the police force, so you offer a fresh perspective."

Dotty blinked. It still amazed her how inclusive Lynn was. Her predecessor had grudgingly allowed Dotty to assist with some investigations, but nobody from the police, apart from Keya, had ever actively sought her input. But then, Lynn wasn't at all territorial or glory-seeking.

She seemed content to focus on solving crimes without worrying about who took the credit. For her, teamwork was at the heart of the process. It was a refreshing approach.

"Sorry about that," said a slightly breathless Keya, who had materialised at their table while Dotty was reflecting on Lynn's attitude.

"Why don't I take your orders for lunch, and then, hopefully, we can sit down and review the case? I think the main lunchtime rush is over."

Dotty chose a couscous salad with sun-dried tomatoes and feta cheese, accompanied by a pot of refreshing mint tea.

Once Keya had taken their orders, she disappeared again.

Lynn turned to Dotty and said, "So, tell me about Beth's inheritance."

"The benefactor was a man called Peter, or Pete Reynolds."

Lynn raised a hand. "Let me stop you there." She turned to Warren. "Is that the same man you've been looking into?"

"Yes," Warren confirmed. "Keya asked me to do so, as she thought there might be a link to our case."

"And what did you discover?"

Warren pulled out his notebook and flicked through the pages. He smoothed one down and began reading. "Peter Reynolds died aged ninety-eight at Cheltenham General Hospital on 22nd January this year."

"So he'd reached a good age," Lynn said. "Was his death due to natural causes?"

"No, it was the result of a fall at a charity event in December. He never fully recovered and suffered complications from a fractured hip, which led to pneumonia."

"That all seems straightforward," Lynn remarked.

"How did he fall?" Dotty asked. "I mean, were there any suspicious circumstances?"

Lynn raised an eyebrow in curiosity.

"Nothing suspicious was reported. But he was…" Warren hesitated, searching for the right words.

"Elderly?" Lynn suggested, giving him a small, understanding smile. "So Peter, or Pete as you call him, died in January, and in his will, he left something of value to Beth. Do we know why, and what the connection was between them?"

"It wasn't a formal will," Dotty explained. "I still need to chase the lawyer to confirm whether the letter of bequest is legally binding. Apparently,

Pete was a regular at The Owl's Nook, initially drawn, I believe, by its collection of military books. Helen started the collection with those of her father, and when Beth found his trunk of wartime memorabilia, she and Pete became close."

"I'm guessing by that, and Pete's age, that he fought in the Second World War," Lynn queried.

"Yes, and amazingly, he served in the same unit that Helen's father commanded. Apparently, they were a small group who called themselves The Little Owls after a foreign interpreter who was also part of the group."

"Do you think that's why Helen was so fond of owls and named her bookshop The Owl's Nook?" Lynn asked.

"That's the conclusion I've come to," Dotty agreed.

"So Beth and Pete bonded over the war, his memories of it, and her - what is he? - her great-grandfather?"

"Yes, that's right. Lieutenant Francis Tyndall."

Warren jotted something in his notebook.

"And what did he leave to Beth?"

"A painting and an owl pendant," Dotty replied as Keya set down a tray with their drinks on it.

"A pendant almost identical to the one I found in the bookshop, which we believe Helen was wearing."

"Oh, that's right. I've seen the evidence log," Lynn confirmed. "And the gold chain you also discovered."

"And the painting Pete had may have an interesting history," Dotty added. "I've asked a specialist to research it. So far, he's discovered it was hanging in a house in East Germany up until the war, but we have no idea how it ended up in Pete's possession."

"He stole it," Keya stated, placing a floral teapot in front of Dotty. "He probably took it as a memento or to prevent someone else from taking or damaging it."

"That's actually a very reasonable explanation," Dotty considered. "It must have been chaotic at the end of the war. We know the Nazis stole countless treasures, but how many more were destroyed by bombs and shells?"

"Or soldiers," Lynn said dryly. "I've visited several historic houses with Emily that required huge restoration work after the war because of the damage soldiers caused. It's as if they couldn't see beyond the destruction, as though there was a compulsion to obliterate everything of value or beauty."

Keya left, carrying the empty tray.

Dotty inclined her head at Lynn, struck by her profound statement. Then she said, "Dr Marston should be able to tell us more about the painting after he's conducted further research."

"And the owl pendant, or pendants. What do we know about them?" Lynn enquired.

"We know the jeweller who created them was a German immigrant called Otto Mond. He appears to have been a skilled craftsman, but from my research, it seems he didn't work through official channels and instead undertook private commissions."

"Does that mean it's going to be difficult to find out more about the owls?" Lynn asked.

"It does, even though Beth told me that her great-grandfather had them commissioned for his unit. They aren't hallmarked, so they won't be registered with the Worshipful Company of Goldsmiths. Do you think they could be significant to your case?"

"At this point, anything could help. How do you suggest we discover more about them?"

"As I said, it won't be easy. But I remember a time when we were researching a diamond necklace with a ruby pendant and found additional information through a curator in the jewellery department at the Victoria and Albert Museum in London."

"So you could contact them," Lynn suggested, "and Warren can help or provide official backup if needed."

"I suppose so," Dotty replied cautiously. Did she have time to assist Lynn and her team with the investigation? Still, she was intrigued by the owl pendants.

She added, "Yes, I'll see who's best to speak to and find out what I can."

"Thank you," Lynn said, as though Dotty was an accepted member of her team, and this task was just part of her role.

Keya returned with Zivah, and they placed dishes on the table. Couscous for Dotty and Keya, soup and a sandwich for Lynn, and a meatball sandwich with avocado, salsa, and cheese for Warren.

"What have I missed?" Keya asked eagerly as she sat down.

CHAPTER TWENTY-SEVEN

KEYA

Keya dipped her fork into her couscous salad. She felt frustrated at missing the start of the discussion between Lynn, Dotty, and Warren, but she'd had to attend to the café's customers first.

As she arrived with the lunches, she'd caught Dotty saying she'd speak to someone and try to find out more. Who and what, Keya wondered, as she asked, "What have I missed?"

"Dotty has agreed to try to discover more about the owl pendants. They're not much of a lead, but at the moment I'll take anything to move this case forward towards a satisfactory conclusion," Lynn replied.

Keya nodded, but not being sure what had already been covered and needing to be clear, she asked, "Can I just confirm you're treating Helen's death as suspicious and believe another party was involved? I've seen the reports, and the blood on the wooden owl matches Helen's. Is there any doubt she was struck with it?"

"Do you mean, could she have fallen against it?" Lynn asked, then shook her head. "I don't see how, since it was found several bookshelves away from where her body lay. There was no evidence she was moved or that she dragged herself across the bookshop, was there?"

"No," Keya confirmed.

"So, if the cause of death was blunt force trauma—most likely from being struck with the owl—then yes, we're treating it as suspicious. In police terms, the working hypothesis is that it was murder."

The answer was what she'd expected, but it mattered to hear it said out loud before they went any further.

And now that the probable cause and place of death were confirmed, the next logical step was to establish opportunity.

She began, “Helen’s body was found in the bookshop by the shop assistant, Nicole Blake, at five fifteen on Saturday afternoon.”

“Right,” Lynn said, giving her a nod to continue.

“And even though it was past closing time, the front door of the bookshop was open, so anyone could have had access.”

“That’s also true,” Lynn agreed. “But Nicole didn’t see anyone else in the bookshop when she arrived. Laura was in the cafe next door, clearing up and waiting for the last table of customers to leave. Warren, you found and spoke to them, didn’t you?”

Warren wiped his sticky fingers on his napkin, but as it was already dirty, Keya passed him hers. His fingers finally clean, Warren turned to another page in his notebook.

“Yes, the Lewis’s and the Tunnell’s. Two couples who’d spent the day cycling and finished it with tea and cake at the cafe. As they were on holiday and live in London, I spoke to both wives over the phone. They confirmed they left the cafe just after five."

"So, before the body was found," Dotty remarked.

"Yes," Lynn responded. "They could have been involved as the timescale fits, except Laura saw them all climb onto their bikes and cycle away."

"The coroner estimated the time of death as up to an hour before the body was found," Keya stated, "based on its temperature and the fact rigor mortis hadn't yet set in."

"So, a quarter past four to quarter past five," Dotty concluded.

"I've expanded the window to four o'clock until five fifteen, as predicting time of death is not an exact science," Lynn added.

"That's sensible. But who exactly does it put in the frame?" enquired Keya.

"Laura. She could easily have sneaked through from the cafe to the bookshop. And Beth was in the house. However, they both seem flummoxed and devastated by Helen's death. We haven't found any reason either of them would have wanted her out of the way, have we, Warren?"

The younger officer shook his head.

"What about Sebastian Henshaw? Nicole accused him of being at the bookshop on Saturday afternoon," Dotty said.

"That's right. And I actually interviewed him myself," Lynn replied.

Keya leaned forward to hear more.

"He was extremely cagey, and I definitely can't rule him out, although attacking Helen would be an extreme way of getting what he wanted."

"Which was?" asked Dotty.

"Someone—he refused to divulge who—had approached him about buying The Owl's Nook, converting the building into flats, and taking the bookshop business online. He said he went to the bookshop on Saturday to try to persuade Helen to sell."

"I shouldn't think that went well," Keya remarked.

"No, I agree. Sebastian became very defensive. But his behaviour seemed to be more about his business proposal being turned down than anything to do with Helen. Still, let's leave that open for now. We need to dig a little deeper into him, his motive, and his alibi, as he swears he left before four."

"Was Nicole definitely away from the bookshop during the time the crime was committed?" Dotty asked. "She was very guarded and surly when we visited Laura and Beth yesterday. I think she resented Helen for appointing Imogen Henshaw to modernise the bookshop's online presence. Not that I'm saying that would be a reason to harm Helen, but there could have been other tensions between them."

Lynn looked to Warren, who said, "I still need to get to the bottom of her alibi."

"So that's two potential suspects," stated Keya. "And then there's Beth's father, and Laura's husband, Declan Reid."

"I don't trust him at all," Lynn admitted. "With his criminal record and evasive behaviour, he is one of my prime suspects, and he was in the area. Warren spoke to a regular at the bookshop who saw him arguing with Helen the week before her death. Declan dismissed it as a minor disagreement, but I don't believe him. My guess is they were arguing about money, especially since we know he is broke and borrowing from friends. It's definitely an avenue we need to explore."

"It seems to me you have several leads," Keya observed. "Is there anyone else of interest we know who was at the bookshop on Saturday afternoon?"

"There's the sporty silver Mercedes," Warren pointed out. "The cyclists saw it drive in as they arrived, but they didn't see who was behind the wheel. Nobody got out of the car while they were sorting out their gear, which they thought was odd. And none of the regular customers I've spoken to owns or recognises a car like that."

Keya nodded. "So that's another lead."

"Yes," Lynn agreed. "I just hope one of them leads us to the culprit."

CHAPTER TWENTY-EIGHT

KEYA

Keya put thoughts about The Owl's Nook and Helen Fletcher's death out of her mind over the weekend, as she was busy with the cafe.

The previous week's showers had given way to sunshine, and customers were even asking to sit outside on the patio overlooking the River Coln. This meant the cafe was busier than ever, with more people to cater for.

"Are you getting up this morning?" Sujin asked, placing a cup of tea on Keya's bedside table on Monday morning.

"What time is it?" she mumbled groggily. She'd

heard Sujin turn on the shower earlier, but she must have drifted back to sleep.

"Quarter to eight," Sujin replied brightly.

Keya squinted at him, noticing that he was fully dressed, clean-shaven, and that his dark, floppy hair was still damp.

"I have to leave soon," he continued. "I was in two minds about waking you, but I wasn't sure if you had any plans for today?"

"The cafe's shut, as usual," she said, pulling the duvet up to her chin. Then she froze. "The cafe. Mine is shut, but they're planning to reopen the one at The Owl's Nook. Oh no," she groaned, "I'm supposed to meet Warren at nine to check the crime scene before handing it over."

"Then you'd better get up." He bent down and kissed her before adding, "I'll see you tonight."

Once Sujin had left, Keya was tempted to roll over and go back to sleep, but her mind was already working through the process of returning the bookshop to Laura Fletcher. She sighed, pulled back the duvet, and slowly swung her legs over the edge of the bed.

Time to get up.

Forty minutes later, Keya drove her metallic reef-blue VW Polo out of Tetbury along the A429, heading towards Cirencester and on to Stow-on-the-Wold.

The sunny morning lifted her spirits, and she turned up Corinium Radio, singing along to Queen's *Don't Stop Me Now* as she cruised along the ancient Roman road.

At The Owl's Nook, Warren was waiting for her, leaning casually against his blue-and-yellow checked police car. He smiled as she pulled in, seemingly unperturbed that she was ten minutes late having spent the last few miles stuck behind a slow-moving tractor.

"Morning. Where do you want to start?" he asked cheerfully as she climbed out of her car.

Grabbing her canvas briefcase from the passenger seat, she replied, "Let's do a final walkthrough of the building. If everything checks out, we can sign everything off and hand it back to Laura. She's expecting us."

Inside, the bookshop was just as she'd left it, although a light film of dust had already settled over the shelves. The room seemed to yearn for activity and for the books to be read, not simply left to sit on their wooden shelves.

She waited while Warren checked the perimeter of the room. When he returned, he nodded and said, "Yeah, everything's as we left it."

"Great. Let's check the cafe, and then we can tell Laura The Owl's Nook is officially hers again," Keya said in a businesslike tone.

"Do you think she'll give up her teaching job?" Warren asked as Keya opened the interconnecting door and moved into the café.

"I've no idea …" Keya started, but her words faltered as she immediately sensed something was wrong.

"What is it?" Warren asked, following her into the room.

"Something's off. Can you feel it?"

"I can feel a breeze, if that's what you mean," Warren replied.

"Let's check the doors."

The one at the far end, leading to the house, was closed but unlocked. Just as Keya was about to investigate further, Warren called out, his voice sharp. "Keya!"

She retraced her steps and crossed the cafe to join him beside a door at the side of the building.

"Someone's forced this open. Look," he said, pointing.

The old wooden door stood ajar. Its dated but robust brass mortice lock was fixed in the closed position. She pulled on a pair of latex gloves before bending down to examine it more closely.

"There are scratches around the keyhole," she observed. "And the plate is loose. Someone's definitely forced it."

"But why?" Warren asked, his brow furrowing.

"To access the bookshop, perhaps? The internal door between the cafe and the shop wasn't locked."

"But we checked, and everything was in its place."

"We only gave it a cursory once-over because we weren't expecting anything unusual," Keya replied, her tone thoughtful. "But now? Perhaps we should check again."

"Do you think this has something to do with the murder?"

"I have no idea," she admitted. "But it does make me wonder if I've missed something. We already have the murder weapon, so what else could someone be looking for?"

"Hello?" A voice called out from the bookshop.

"That's Laura," Keya said, glancing towards the sound.

"What are you going to tell her?"

"I'm not sure yet. Why don't you take a closer look round here while I speak to her?"

Keya left Warren in the cafe and walked through to the bookshop, her eyes scanning the shelves. What had she missed?

"Hi," she greeted Laura, who was standing with Nicole Blake in the entrance porch. "We …"

"Keya!"

Warren's voice cut through the bookshop, stopping her mid-sentence. What now? Had she overlooked something else?

She gave Laura and Nicole an apologetic smile as Warren shouted, "I think some books have been stolen!"

"What?" Nicole demanded, brushing past Keya and striding quickly through the bookshop towards the cafe.

Laura's eyes widened in alarm.

Keya quickly explained, "While we were checking that everything was in order before handing the shop back to you, we discovered the side door to the cafe had been forced open. We were just trying to figure out why when you arrived."

Unsure of what else to say, she added, "Shall we see what my colleague has found?"

Laura nodded, and together they returned to the cafe. Nicole was crouching beside a low bookshelf situated between two of the cafe's wooden tables.

"Don't touch the ones on the floor," Warren warned as Nicole reached for a large, slim hardback with a glossy cover that gleamed in the light.

"Is anything missing?" Laura asked, her tone full of concern.

"I think so, but I can't tell without checking," Nicole replied, her jaw clenching with frustration.

Keya knelt beside Nicole. Still wearing her gloves, she picked up the three books lying haphazardly on the floor and examined them. They were all comic annuals with dark, dystopian covers, titled *Steel Sentinels*.

"These are part of a collection we acquired last year with other books and comics from a house clearance," Nicole explained. "I don't know much about them. Helen just asked me to find somewhere to display them."

"*Steel Sentinels*," Warren said thoughtfully. He was also wearing gloves and picked up one of the books and flicked through it as he said, "This is one of the later editions."

"I think we had earlier ones too," Nicole said, tilting her head to read the spines of the books still on the shelf.

"The earliest editions are rare," Warren said knowledgeably.

Keya gave him an appreciative look before asking, "And valuable?" Her thoughts shifted to the possibility that this break-in might not be connected to Helen's death after all.

"Sure, but not as much as the 1981 annual featuring Captain Crucible's debut. And then there's the 1987 special deluxe edition. I've only seen pictures of it, but it has a black cover with gold-foil lettering."

"There might have been one of those in the collection," Nicole said, her brow furrowing.

"Does this mean we can't reopen the bookshop?" Laura asked, her shoulders slumping.

Keya considered the question before replying. “This incident seems limited to the cafe. Why don’t I go back to the bookshop with you while Nicole gives Warren all the details she can about the comic annuals and the door that was forced open?”

CHAPTER TWENTY-NINE

KEYA

Keya left Warren with Nicole Blake to investigate the apparent break-in at The Owl's Nook cafe and accompanied Laura Fletcher back into the bookshop.

She began, "I'm happy to hand the bookshop area back, but..."

"Please, don't worry," Laura interjected. "I'm as keen as you are to figure out who broke into the cafe and what was stolen. It looks like upgrading our security needs to be added to the list of improvements needed to modernise our business."

"What else are you planning to do?" Keya enquired, genuinely interested.

"Imogen Henshaw, who's coming this morning, has some fantastic ideas for building a more marketable online presence. The physical shop has been slowly declining, but the cafe remains popular. I'm wondering whether we should extend it into the bookshop or introduce a range of more profitable non-book related items."

This was an area of business Keya understood. Her cafe was busy, and she had run a deli for a while.

Initially, it had been popular, but trade had eventually died down, mainly due to their remote location. The Owl's Nook, however, was on the edge of a bustling market town.

"I can see that working," Keya agreed. "Now, let's sort out the paperwork."

Laura was just signing her name when Imogen appeared at the bookshop entrance.

"Hi," she said. "Can I come in?"

Keya gathered the papers together and said to Laura, "It's all yours. Are you opening today?"

"No, we weren't sure if we could. Besides, this gives us a chance to really go through Imogen's proposals." Laura nodded to the younger woman, who stepped inside.

Laura and Imogen began discussing plans as Keya packed the signed documents into her briefcase. When she looked up, Warren and Nicole were walking across the bookshop towards her.

"Everything okay?" Keya asked.

"Nicole is certain some annuals are missing. If you've handed back the bookshop, she can start checking for them?" Warren replied.

"Most of the second-hand books are still recorded in a paper filing system," Nicole explained. "Helen preferred it that way."

"Speaking of paper and files..." Warren turned to Keya with a questioning look.

She narrowed her eyes. "What about them?"

"I couldn't make head or tail of the ones Imogen gave us last week."

A flicker of satisfaction crossed Nicole's face, but it vanished when Imogen offered, "Shall I go through them with you?"

"Is that okay?" Warren asked, glancing at Keya as though seeking her approval, despite her no longer officially being a police sergeant.

"Yes, it sounds very sensible," Keya agreed. "And I need to secure the cafe."

Leaving the bookshop, she headed to her car, where she kept various useful items, including a roll of police tape. Walking around the outside of the building, she cordoned off the damaged doorway and placed a 'Police - Stop' sign beside it.

Satisfied, but knowing it was only a temporary measure, she returned to the bookshop.

"So, what we have here," Imogen explained as Keya walked through the stone entrance porch, "are orders or deliveries for these items."

"And what are they?" Warren asked, his gaze fixed intently on Imogen.

"For that, we'll need to look at more of the deleted files I uncovered over the weekend."

At the far end of the counter, Keya noticed Nicole stiffen. In fact, every time the files were mentioned, Nicole seemed uneasy.

On a hunch, Keya asked, “Nicole, what do you know about the deleted files?”

“I… what?” Nicole stammered, dropping the index card she was holding.

Laura, who was sorting papers midway down the counter, turned to stare at Nicole, whose face flushed crimson.

Bingo! thought Keya.

Laura, her suspicion evident, asked in a probing tone, “Nicole, what is this about? Is this why you and Mum kept arguing?”

So, Nicole and Helen’s relationship hadn’t been as smooth as they’d been led to believe, Keya realised.

“No… I mean, maybe,” Nicole stammered before blurting, “She knew nothing about it. But how was I supposed to live on what she paid me? I had to find a way to make more money.”

Keya stepped closer and asked, “By doing what?”

“Taking orders for books and pamphlets. Nothing serious,” Nicole muttered.

"Through the bookshop?" Laura pressed, leaning towards Nicole.

Keya noticed Warren pick up his pen as he and Imogen turned their full attention to Nicole, who gave a hesitant nod.

"I don't understand. Why do it separately from the bookshop?" Laura pressed.

"Because it wasn't the sort of stuff Helen would sell, OK?" Nicole snapped defensively, shoving an index card back into its box.

At the computer, Imogen tapped a few keys and then said in a cautious tone, "No, I don't suppose they were."

Warren, leaned closer to look at the screen.

"Oh!" he exclaimed. "I'm not sure that's actually legal."

Keya narrowed her eyes at Nicole. "What exactly were these books and pamphlets about?"

Nicole turned away, pretending to focus on removing another index card from the box.

"*The Iron Doctrine* by Victor Krieg," Warren read aloud. "It calls for violent revolution and racial purity, denounces democracy as corrupt, and glorifies terrorism. It's banned in the UK for inciting hatred and serving as a rallying cry for extremists."

Keya's gaze intensified on Nicole's back as Laura exclaimed, "No wonder you didn't want Mum to know about this. She'd never have agreed to sell something like that in the bookshop."

Nicole spun around, her voice defensive and tense as she blurted, "Of course, I knew that! Why do you think I kept it separate? I didn't want her or the shop getting into trouble. But when she refused to let me make changes to modernise the bookshop, I had to find another way to earn money. And not everything I sold was illegal. They were just things Helen wouldn't have approved of..."

Her voice faltered, and she dropped her gaze to the floor.

"Did she find out?" Keya asked, her tone probing.

Nicole's head jerked up. "Oh, I hope not! Do you think she did?" Panic crept into her voice.

"What Keya means," Laura said perceptively, "is did Mum discover your side business, and did it lead to arguments between you?"

Nicole hesitated before admitting, "No, I'm sure she didn't."

"But you did argue?" Keya pressed.

"Look, I'm twenty-four. I've worked here for six years, and at first, it was exciting. I loved it when Helen trusted me to run the shop on my own. But that's all it's ever been. A small bookshop. Sure, we made some changes, like adding more second-hand books, and I enjoyed going to auctions and house clearances with her. But eventually, she stopped taking me, leaving me to manage the shop instead."

"Why didn't you leave?" Keya asked. "And find another job?"

"Doing what?" Nicole's voice was strained. "My dad has mental health issues. Sometimes he's fine, but other times he's depressed and withdrawn. After Mum left, I was the one who had to take care of him and my younger brother. With Dad unable to hold down a job, my salary is vital. I even work three nights a week at The Bell, but it's still not enough to cover everything."

"Why didn't you tell us?" Laura asked gently.

Nicole shrugged, her posture defensive. "It's my problem, not yours."

"This is a family business," Laura replied, her tone calm yet firm. "And you're part of that family. Whatever outdated ideas you, or your dad, might have about keeping things private shouldn't have stopped you from asking us for help. What you've been doing for your family is admirable, but the responsibility shouldn't fall on you alone."

Keya nodded, agreeing with Laura, although she understood how hard it could be to act on such advice when caught in those situations.

Laura continued, "If you want more responsibility, that's great. I don't want to give up my teaching completely. I've already cut back my hours to oversee the cafe. If you're willing to help manage that and implement the changes we're working on with Imogen, I'd be grateful. And, of course, the role would come with a significant pay rise."

Nicole bit her lip, her fingers tugging at her brown jumper as she stared uncertainly at Laura.

Laura gave her an encouraging smile.

“What about the pamphlets and books I’ve been selling?” Nicole asked hesitantly, her voice tinged with worry and remorse.

Imogen, still seated at the computer, pressed a key dramatically. “What books and pamphlets?” she asked innocently.

“Oi! Where did they go?” Warren exclaimed, craning his neck to peer at the screen.

“OK,” Keya said firmly, trying to calm the situation. “Constable Sparrow has more important things to do right now than track down every book and pamphlet you sold.”

Warren’s frown conveyed that he disagreed, but Keya pressed on. “What we need to focus on is your alibi for Saturday afternoon. Were your deliveries connected to this side business?”

Nicole nodded reluctantly.

“Then we’ll need a list of the places you visited for Constable Sparrow to follow up,” Keya said.

"And make sure none of your customers are involved in anything illegal," Warren added pointedly.

Nicole's eyes widened, so Keya softened her tone as she said, "Don't worry. While Warren's right to investigate, it's unlikely your customers are extremists. But your other venture needs to stop. Immediately."

Nicole nodded again, wiping her nose with her sleeve.

"And you'll provide the delivery list from Saturday?" Keya prompted.

Nicole hesitated, her gaze darting to Laura, who offered another reassuring smile.

"OK," Nicole said finally.

"Great. Warren," Keya instructed, "can you take Nicole's formal statement?"

CHAPTER THIRTY

DOTTY

On Monday morning, Dotty was relieved to find that there had been no further disasters or untoward events at Akemans over the weekend.

A few stallholders were already setting up for the week and they greeted her cheerfully as she passed through the main auction room to the rear office.

It almost felt as though the stalls had always been there. Their presence added energy to the space, and she felt a renewed sense of optimism as she entered the office and switched on the lights.

In a normal month, she'd be busy preparing for Akemans' auction, but the one at Cirencester Auctioneers wasn't until the following week. Still, she needed to check the condition reports she and Amanda had written so Clara could send them out when customers requested them.

More importantly, she needed to drum up business for the following month's auction to ensure that it went ahead, although she had no idea where they would actually hold it. But that was something she could work out with Gilly and Zach once she had sufficient lots to hold a sale.

She made a mental note to ask Marion to reach out to her contact at Akemans' estate agency. Probate cases, house clearances, and downsizing clients often yielded items for auctions, and Dotty was determined to make May's auction work.

At least Marion had persuaded the man Dotty had met at The Owl's Nook on the evening of Hugo's presentation to submit a few quality lots. She'd visited him the previous Tuesday, and if they sold well, she was confident he had more items to sell.

Opening her emails, Dotty was interested to find one from the lawyer confirming that Pete's letter of bequest was legal. She forwarded a copy to Beth and Laura Fletcher, and another to Pete's nephew, whose initial response to the news of the bequest had been indifference, perhaps because he had no idea of the value of the two items.

With this complete, she decided her next job should be to contact the jewellery expert at the Victoria and Albert Museum.

His contact details were in their system, so she wrote an email describing Pete's owl pendant, as well as Helen's, and the other information she'd been told about them. It wasn't much, she reflected as she pressed send, but perhaps she'd learn more as a result of the email.

"Good afternoon, Akemans auction house," Clara said politely as she picked up the ringing telephone. After a brief pause, she added, "Certainly. May I ask who's calling?"

Covering the mouthpiece, she called across to Dotty, who was deliberating which photos to include with a condition report for a set of eight balloon-backed mahogany dining chairs, and said, "Professor Ross from the V&A."

"Really? That's quick," Dotty responded before picking up the phone on her desk. "Good afternoon, Professor."

"Is that Miss Sayers?"

"Mrs Sayers, but please call me Dotty."

"Of course, and how is Bernadette?" So, the professor was a friend of Aunt Beanie's.

"Very well, thank you."

"Good, good. Now, I received your email, and as I'm flying to Munich later this week, I wanted to deal with it today. Also, I admit, items like your owls always fascinate me."

"Have you been able to find out much?" Dotty enquired.

"A little, although I can't really take the credit. A similar request was received by our department eight years ago," Professor Ross revealed.

"Really? For another owl?"

"Yes, and I was able to see from the image on file that it was similar but not exactly the same as your two. It had one red and one orange eye."

"Oh, that's interesting. And what did you discover about it?" enquired Dotty.

"We have Otto Mond's journal," revealed the professor. "According to the file, a colleague of mine went through it and found that a total of six owls were made from a gold chalice with inlaid jewels, which was melted down. The chalice was provided by a Lieutenant Francis Tyndall, who commissioned the pendants in 1948."

"I'm aware of Francis Tyndall," Dotty replied enthusiastically. "One of the pendants I sent an image of was found in a trunk of his belongings, recently discovered by his great-granddaughter. And she thought he'd had them commissioned for members of his wartime unit."

"And the other belonged to a client of yours, Peter Reynolds?" Professor Ross asked.

"That's right, or at least it came from his house. He died earlier this year, but we think he served alongside Francis Tyndall during the war, and that's why he had a pendant."

"It's certainly possible, although I don't have any records of who the pendants were given to. In fact, that's all we have on file. I presume you'd like to know their value?"

"Yes, of course," Dotty responded, sinking back into her chair. Her initial excitement at discovering that Beth's great-grandfather had arranged for six pendants to be made had faded into disappointment. Was this all they were going to uncover?

"On their own, we estimate each is worth £3,000 to £5,000. However, if you could bring the whole set together, their value would rise to at least £50,000. Any related items belonging to Lieutenant Tyndall, Peter Reynolds, or the other recipients that add to their story would increase the value even further."

This was as Dotty had expected, knowing that personal items backing up the provenance or story of artefacts always increased their appeal to collectors. But she still couldn't quite shake the deflated feeling that lingered after her initial optimism.

"Thank you for your help," she said, trying to sound as if she meant it.

"I'd be interested to hear if you find the other owls," said Professor Ross.

"Of course, but I doubt we will, unless we discover another lead."

"Good luck with that, and thank you. This has been an interesting distraction from my day job. But I must be getting on," said Professor Ross.

"Thank you," replied Dotty. "Oh, and one more thing…"

But the professor had ended the call.

The question she'd wanted to ask was who had enquired about a pendant eight years ago.

As she slowly replaced the telephone receiver, Clara said brightly, "The professor's call reminded me that I still had one more folder of Pete Reynolds' papers to go through." Tapping a manilla file on her desk she continued, "Most of it is letters, with a few newspaper cuttings, but I also found a photo I thought you might be interested in."

Clara stood up and walked across to Dotty's desk, placing a grainy black-and-white photo on it. One corner was ripped, and it was slightly faded, but it was still possible to see the group of uniformed men.

Turning the photo over, Dotty read, "Saxony, 1945".

She studied the photo again. There were five uniformed men. The tall one at the side wearing a peaked cap looked to be in charge. Was that Francis Tyndall? On the other side was a small man—more of a boy, really—who wore a jumper with a hole in the arm and a broad smile.

"I wonder if this is the unit they called The Little Owls, and if that's Helen's father," said Dotty, pointing to the taller man. "I presume the young man who's not in uniform is the interpreter. Which one do you think is Pete?"

"I've no idea," Clara replied, "but I still have some letters to read through. Shall I do that now, in case any of them mention the photograph?"

"If you could, that would be great. Then we'll know we've been through everything. I might call Laura Fletcher about her grandfather's trunk.

Maybe there are more letters or photos in there that could help us."

Dotty then replayed the full conversation she'd had with Professor Ross.

"Don't be too disappointed," Clara said encouragingly. "It's another step forward, and a further link between the pendants, Beth's great-grandfather, and Pete."

She smiled reassuringly before returning to her desk.

Dotty found the number for the bookshop and dialled it.

"The Owl's Nook," answered a voice Dotty thought was Nicole's. Was the shop open again?

"Hello, this is Dotty Sayers from Akemans auction house. Can I speak to Laura?"

"One moment, please," Nicole replied, sounding efficient but not particularly warm.

Dotty waited for Laura to come to the phone.

After a few minutes, Laura said, "Hello. Is this about Beth's inheritance? I saw your email."

"I'm pleased the lawyer has confirmed it, but I'm still researching the items."

"I thought you said that would be expensive."

"This is partly for Beth and partly for the police. They've asked me to look into the owl pendants, because your mother was wearing one the afternoon she died, which is why I'm calling. Beth mentioned finding her great-grandfather's trunk with his wartime possessions, and I wondered if there were any letters or photographs among them that might help with our research?"

"I've certainly seen some photographs. There's one of my Grandfather, looking very dashing, and another of him and his friends. There were also some sketches which Beth stuck in a scrapbook to protect them. I'm not sure about any letters, but you can certainly come and have a look."

"Can I? That would be great." Dotty checked her watch. It was five past three. "Would you mind if I came over now?"

CHAPTER THIRTY-ONE

DOTTY

Dotty arrived at The Owl's Nook just before four o'clock, and hooked a small black bag over her shoulder which held Pete's grainy photograph of the soldiers in Saxony.

She hoped her research wouldn't take too long, or that Laura wouldn't mind her staying past closing time if it did.

As she approached the entrance porch, she noticed the duck-egg blue door was closed. Perhaps the bookshop wasn't open, and she should try the house instead.

As she hesitated, unsure of what to do, the door opened, and Imogen Henshaw stepped out.

Smiling, Imogen held the door open for Dotty, who thanked her before moving into the porch.

The same leaflets she'd seen on her first visit, advertising local Cotswold attractions, drooped in their wooden holder.

Inside, the bookshop gleamed. A humming sound drew Dotty's attention to her right, where Laura was manoeuvring a round-fronted floor polisher. Spotting Dotty, Laura switched off the machine and walked over to greet her.

"When do you open?" Dotty asked.

"Wednesday, hopefully. Not that we've told many customers. We didn't want to until the police had handed the place back, and then we weren't sure how much mess there would be. But we've made great progress today, haven't we, Nicole?"

Nicole, tapping away at a laptop keyboard, stopped and smiled. "It'll only take me an hour or so to finish dusting the books tomorrow, and then we can start on the cafe."

"If we're allowed to clean it," Laura added dejectedly.

"Why wouldn't you be?" Dotty enquired.

"Because the police discovered someone had broken in and stolen some comics."

"Comics?" Dotty repeated, surprised. Of all the things to steal, she hadn't expected that.

"Annuals, really, and according to the young constable, they may actually be valuable. Mum missed a trick there."

"So the cafe is now a crime scene?"

"Keya's finished examining the door, so at least we can secure that, but there's still the area around the bookshelf where the comics, or annuals, were. It might be better if we go through the house to reach the storeroom where my grandfather's trunk is kept."

Dotty followed Laura, emerging at the rear of the cafe, near the kitchen.

"I hope it's all right to come in here and to show you the trunk."

"I have been asked by Inspector Lynn to discover what I can about the owl pendants," Dotty told her.

"Then I'm sure it'll be fine." Laura said as she opened a small door and held it open for Dotty. Inside the walk-in cupboard were several boxes of books and a faded green tin trunk with Francis Tyndall's name on it.

"Can you find your way back?" Laura asked. "I'd like to finish polishing the floor and return the equipment tonight."

"Yes, of course," Dotty replied distractedly, already captivated by the trunk and what it might contain.

The scrapbook Laura had mentioned was at the top. Dotty slowly flicked through its pages, admiring the pencil sketches of houses, villages, and bomb-damaged towns. Owl doodles appeared repeatedly.

At the back, she stopped. One page featured a sketch of items that appeared to be paintings, furniture, and wooden crates. Opposite was a drawing of what looked like a chalice, with darker marks hinting at gems.

Could this be the one Francis Tyndall had melted down to create the owl pendants? But where had it come from? Had he discovered it during the war?

Nazi treasure, perhaps, and if so, were the other items part of the same hoard?

She set the scrapbook aside. It deserved closer examination, and it might interest either Hugo or Professor Ross.

Next, her attention was drawn to a wooden box with mother-of-pearl inlay and a tree surrounded by Hebrew script on the lid. Inside was a photograph of a tall young man in military uniform, wearing a peaked cap.

Dotty retrieved Pete's photograph from her bag and compared the two. The same man appeared in both images. The officer she assumed was Lieutenant Francis Tyndall.

Another photograph showed a group of soldiers standing in front of a large, partially damaged house with ornate windows and a steeply pitched roof, unmistakably European in style.

Comparing the photographs, Dotty noted that the young man in civilian clothes appeared only in Pete's photo, while a slightly chubby soldier had replaced him in Francis's. Perhaps the missing men in each photo were the ones who had taken them.

She turned over the group photo from Francis's box and read, 'Hirschfeld Haus. Myself with the boys. Pete, Walt, Bert, Matt, Rob'.

Were these the men who called themselves The Little Owls? Spotting a stylised owl doodle in the bottom left corner, she thought they might be.

Searching the box further, Dotty found several interesting items, including a metal medallion bearing a swastika, but no letters or papers about The Little Owls or Francis's military unit.

Still, from the back of Pete's photo she had a location—Saxony—and from the back of Francis's, most of the soldiers' first names. They were small clues, but they might lead to more.

Carefully, she packed everything back into the trunk, except for the scrapbook and photographs, which she placed in her bag alongside Pete's photo. As she closed and secured the trunk, her phone rang.

"Hi, Clara. Is everything OK?" she asked, her heart beating a little faster. Couldn't she leave the office for a few hours without there being an incident?

"Oh yes, but I found something you might be interested in and I wasn't sure if you werc coming back."

Dotty checked her watch. Five to five. "I wasn't planning to, but what have you discovered?"

"A letter among Pete's papers referring to a reunion and the issuing of the owl pendants."

"Excellent!" Dotty exclaimed, the sound startlingly loud in the small room. "Can you leave it out? I've also found something. Maybe together they'll help us piece together the history of the pendants."

CHAPTER THIRTY-TWO

DOTTY

Dotty was surprised to find Clara still working in the office when she returned to Akemans on Monday evening at twenty to six.

"Have you been waiting for me?" she asked, hanging her blue padded jacket on the wooden coat stand.

"Yes. I wanted to show you what I've found and see what you've discovered. It feels like we're finally starting to make sense of why the pendants were important."

Dotty placed the scrapbook on Clara's desk. "This contains Francis Tyndall's sketches," she said, removing Pete's photograph from her bag along with the other two she'd found in the trunk. She laid them out side by side on the desk.

"There are names on the back of this one," she explained, tapping the photograph of the men in front of the war-damaged house.

"I wonder…" Clara mused, standing and walking to the desk Dotty had claimed as her own. "I found this letter among Pete's papers today." She picked up a yellowing page and said, "It was written by someone called Walt, who lived in Manchester in 1948."

"Didn't the man whose daughter sold his painting at Barnaby's in Bicester live in Manchester? And wasn't his name Walter?"

"Yes," Clara replied, returning to her desk with the letter and pressing a key on her computer. The screen came to life, and she scanned it. "Walter Jameson. His daughter was Hayley. They sold a Josef Stoitzner painting in 1998 for £16,000."

Dotty turned the photograph over, rereading the names on the back. "Walt," she muttered, turning it face up again. "I wonder which one he is. And we still don't know which is Pete."

"There's more in the letter," Clara said, picking it up. "Walt writes about a reunion of The Little Owls ..."

"Finally, an actual reference to them!" Dotty interjected, then quickly apologised. "Sorry, I didn't mean to interrupt."

"That's OK." Clara smiled before continuing.

"He said it was a shame Matt couldn't join them. He hopes he received the owl the boss sent and mentions that maybe Matt will make the next reunion. Then he writes about the young lads, Bert and Rob, saying he hopes they manage to sort themselves out. He acknowledges how hard it's been to settle back into normal life and says he misses his chums in the unit."

Clara paused and looked at Dotty.

"I can't imagine what it must have been like coming back from war," Dotty said. "Four years away... everyone back home would have changed, and so would he. And back then, nobody understood PTSD and things like that."

"You're right," Clara said nodding. "And here's the part that really caught my attention. Walt writes about 'the picture'. He says he looks at it every day to remind himself of the times they spent together. He mentions how they had to leave the Deer House when the 'Russkies' began moving in and their orders came to pull out and return to England."

Dotty picked up the photo of the group of men in front of the house again and turned it over. She considered the notation on the back and asked Clara, "Can you look up Hirschfeld Haus and see if you can find out what it means?"

Clara tapped a few keys as she leaned over her keyboard. She stared at the monitor and read aloud, "Deerfield House."

"Deer House. Deerfield House. Do you think they're the same?"

"Oh, I do," Clara agreed, picking up Walt's letter again. "And listen to this. 'I know we felt like a right bunch of thieves, but did you hear what the Russkies did to the place after we left? Looted it bare and then torched it. Typical, eh? Makes you wonder what they'd have done if they'd found the stash. Glad we got it out of there when we did.

Mind you, I've often wondered what happened to it all after we handed it over.

"Think any of it ended up with the proper owners? Or is it just sitting in some fancy museum somewhere, with no one the wiser? And did you clock the boss's face when someone asked him where he got the gold for our owls? Didn't press him on it, but I reckon he kept a bit of the stash for himself. Can't say I blame him, though'."

"I wonder what that means?" Dotty mused aloud. "It sounds like the Russians were advancing, so the British soldiers withdrew, leaving Deerfield House behind. But when they left, they took some items with them rather than let the Russians get hold of them."

"What kind of items, do you think?" Clara asked, her eyes sparkling with curiosity.

"Paintings, by the sounds of it. And a gold chalice, which I think is the item Bert wondered about in his letter. The one Francis Tyndall kept and later gave to Otto Mond to create the owl pendants. And if there was a gold chalice..." Dotty's words trailed off as she turned the scrapbook toward her and flipped to the back pages.

“I think this is the chalice.” She tapped the sketched image. “And this,” she said, pointing to the pencil drawing opposite, “might be more valuable items.”

“Nazi treasure?” Clara suggested, her voice tinged with excitement.

Dotty smiled indulgently at her. “I’m not sure about that. But I think we should share everything we’ve discovered with Dr Marston and see if it helps his research.”

“And the treasure?” Clara pressed.

Dotty smiled and replied, “I’ll ask him about that too, if you like.”

CHAPTER THIRTY-THREE

KEYA

On Tuesday morning, Lynn and Warren joined Keya at The Owl's Nook cafe.

"So, what does Laura think has been taken?" Lynn asked, eyeing the stack of *Steel Sentinels* comic annuals Warren had placed on top of a small bookshelf.

"Nicole confirmed they're missing a hardback edition from 1987, which Warren believes is valuable," Keya replied.

Lynn glanced at Warren, who nodded seriously.

"They're also missing one from 1985, which Warren thinks could be significant if it features a character called Captain Crucible. That edition was banned due to a controversial story. Annuals from 1980 and 1982 are gone too, and they may have some value as early editions of the series."

"This doesn't sound like an opportunist thief," Lynn reflected. "It seems like someone who knew the bookshop, what they stocked, and exactly where to find these pieces. But I'm surprised they were displayed here if they were worth so much."

"Nicole admitted they didn't know they were," Keya explained. "Helen nearly threw them out, since they don't usually stock comics and that sort of thing. But Nicole persuaded her to keep them and put them in here with the other second-hand books, rather than in the main bookshop. It's likely only a few people would have seen them."

"But those 'few people' could include anyone who's visited the cafe," Lynn pointed out.

"Yes," Keya agreed.

Lynn glanced around before asking, "But why now? Why break in through a sturdy door instead of waiting for the cafe to reopen? The thief could have bought the comics legitimately for, what, a couple of pounds each. Why go to the trouble of stealing them?"

"Maybe they worried that with Helen's death, there'd be a reorganisation of stock or the staff might realise the comics' value," Keya suggested.

She continued, "You know how it is? Once you learn something, you assume everyone else knows it too. So, rather than leave the valuable annuals gathering dust, they saw an opportunity while the cafe was quiet. And even though the door is sturdy, the lock is old, and there are no other security measures. If they knew what they were doing and where to find the comics, they could have been in and out in twenty minutes, or less."

"I presume it's not worth asking if they left any forensic evidence?" Lynn asked.

"I only found smudged prints on the door, so I assume the culprit wore gloves. There was a partial footprint, from which I'd surmise we're looking for a man, or a woman who wears size ten trainers."

"Is there anything else you'll be able to find out from examining the scene?" Lynn asked.

"No. Warren and I both worked on it yesterday. It's a public space, but because it's been empty for a week, there's a layer of dust on most surfaces. As far as I can tell, the thief broke in through the side door, went straight to this bookshelf, removed the books they wanted, discarded the others, and left."

"And the books they discarded?"

"I haven't dusted or tested them for fingerprints. I wasn't sure it was worth it since we know the culprit wore gloves."

"You're probably right," Lynn sighed. "I really don't see how we can catch them based solely on the crime scene. It might be better to focus on where the thief can sell the comics. I've never heard of *Steel Sentinels*."

"They have a cult following," Keya said, glancing at Warren.

He cleared his throat and said, "I could check some of the dealers I know, and sites like eBay and others dedicated to comics and graphic novels."

"That sounds like the best approach. Does this mean we can hand the cafe back?" Lynn asked. "I'd like to be done with this crime scene, even if we can't close either case yet."

"I'll make a few more checks," Keya replied, "and then complete the paperwork with Laura." She glanced into her bag to ensure she had the relevant documents.

"And now that we've cleared Nicole of Helen's death," she continued, "and neither Laura nor Beth appear to have credible motives, who does that leave as your prime suspects? Declan Reid, for one, I guess?"

"He's the main one. Sebastian Henshaw still hasn't given me a satisfactory explanation of his movements, but I'm not sure why he'd want to harm Helen."

"So you're focusing on Declan?"

"I am. And finding the sporty silver Mercedes."

CHAPTER THIRTY-FOUR

DOTTY

Dotty visited Cirencester Auctioneers on Tuesday morning to help Amanda arrange items for the upcoming sale.

"I heard a rumour that you're planning to modernise Akemans and create a bespoke auction room," said Amanda as she effortlessly lifted a cardboard box, containing a collection of pottery jugs of various sizes, and placed it on the second shelf of a free-standing unit near the entrance of the large, converted aircraft hangar.

Surprised, Dotty picked up another box containing white tableware. "Where did you hear that?" she asked, struggling to lift the box onto the first shelf. Once it was in place, she turned to Amanda, who shrugged and waited patiently for an answer.

Dotty sighed, pursing her lips. Then she admitted, "The old mill has some serious structural issues. We've had to move some of the stalls from the antique centre into the auction house until the necessary repairs are carried out. It's a big investment, but since we have to do the work anyway, Zach suggested upgrading both the auction house and the antique centre."

"I think that's a great idea. I love what Barnaby's in Bicester has done with their mezzanine areas. They've got dedicated space for current sales and display areas for future ones. I think they're up to six auctions a month."

"Wow, that's a lot," Dotty replied, wondering if Akemans would ever have enough business to hold multiple sales each month.

"I'd love to do something like that here, but it's so expensive, and I'm not sure it would be worth it. In fact…" Amanda hesitated as Dotty placed two table lamps, which were missing their shades, on the top shelf.

"What?" Dotty asked.

"I've had another offer to buy this building, and I think I'm going to accept it."

"Really?" Dotty said, turning to Amanda, who nodded.

"I've really appreciated your help, and I've enjoyed it when you, Clara, or Marion are around. But when you're not, I'm here by myself. It's lonely, and managing everything for one sale a month just isn't fulfilling anymore."

"What will you do?" Dotty enquired.

"I viewed a country house at the weekend. It's huge and needs a lot of work, but restoring an old property has always been my dream. I want to bring it back to life and give it a new purpose. Maybe I'll turn it into a hotel or split it into apartments. Julia even suggested a retreat, which sounds lovely."

"And you'll use the money from selling this to fund it?"

"Exactly. Why keep working here on something I'm not enjoying?"

"It makes sense," Dotty agreed. Amanda had worked hard to keep Cirencester Auctioneers running with support from the team at Akemans, but Dotty had her own challenges and needed to focus on her business to ensure its survival.

Amanda would once again be left to manage the auctions alone, and the building must be quite valuable now that it was surrounded by an entire industrial estate.

"When will you close?" Dotty asked.

"Since I've finally decided to sell, as soon as possible. Which is why I was wondering if you could include the lots entered for May's auction in your one, if you're holding it?"

"We intend to," Dotty replied, fiddling with the plug on another table lamp. "Although I'm not sure where."

"If the sale hasn't gone through, you might be able to use this building. But…"

"Let's see what happens," Dotty suggested, not wanting to commit to anything just yet.

They continued sorting through auction items, and arranging them on the shelves. After about an hour, Dotty's phone rang and she recognised Hugo's number.

"Hi," she said, answering the call. "Did you get my message?"

"I certainly did. I saw it last night, and I must admit, I haven't been to bed since."

"You've been up all night? Is it that compelling?" Dotty asked, raising her eyebrows in surprise.

"It is to me. I've come across mentions of The Deer House or The Deerpark House, as you've discovered, in other documents and conversations, but I've never been able to determine why it was significant. It was destroyed during the Russian advance into East Germany, and now you have a photograph of it along with references to items stored there. I'm following some leads and waiting for a response from the MOD. Wouldn't it be incredible if we could connect the property to stolen Nazi treasures?"

"It certainly would," Dotty agreed, "and to the owl pendants and Pete's painting."

"Ah yes, of course. Now, I'd like to see the sketches, the letter, and the photographs for myself. Will you be in the office this afternoon?"

"I can be. I'm helping with an auction on the other side of Cirencester at the moment."

"How about mid-afternoon, around three?"

"Yes, I can be back by then."

"And hopefully, I'll have heard back from my MOD contact by then as well."

Dotty continued helping Amanda until half past one, and then she said, "I should let you take a break for lunch, and I need to head back to Akemans to meet Hugo Marston."

"We've made great headway, and my part-time porter will be in tomorrow to help move the heavier items. But when will I see you again?" Amanda tried to sound casual, but there was an appealing note to her voice.

"I'm not sure. I could try to come over on Thursday. Then we can go through the items you already have for May's sale and work on some wording for new enquiries to let people know it will be held at Akemans." She crossed her fingers briefly, hoping that would indeed be the case.

The drive back to Akemans was uneventful, although Dotty enjoyed the short stretch through the Cotswold Water Park. The series of man-made lakes, formed from abandoned gravel quarries, were surrounded by houses in some parts, while other lakes were used for various water sports.

She smiled as she spotted two people in wetsuits propelling themselves across one of the lakes on paddle boards.

Back at Akemans' auction office, she took out the sandwiches she'd made for lunch. She bit into one just as Zach walked into the office.

"You're back," he said, striding towards her desk.

Dotty nodded her response, her mouth full of homemade chicken tikka sandwich filling.

"Oh, that smells good," he remarked.

Dotty swallowed and then offered him the Tupperware container. "Have one. I won't eat them all."

"Thanks," Zach replied, taking a brown bread roll filled with the same chicken tikka mix. "I've been with the structural engineer and an architect all morning. I was going to ask if you wanted to grab lunch at the cafe, but this works just as well."

"What did they say about your proposals?" Dotty asked before taking another bite of her sandwich.

"They said the opening I wanted was too big for the wall, so I need to come up with an alternative. Probably a larger mezzanine in here, with a doorway-sized opening in the party wall. There's plenty of space on the first floor of the old mill, but the engineer advised reinforcing the entire area we want to use, which will add to the cost."

"Is it better to do all the work now?" Dotty mumbled through her food.

"That's the conundrum," agreed Zach waving his sandwich in the air. "Strengthening the entire first floor makes sense, but it's a big investment,"

Clara and Marion entered the office, chatting contentedly as Dotty and Zach continued to discuss the building works. Finally, Dotty asked, "Will you have plans drawn up for both options and get them priced?"

"I think so. It means more consultancy fees, but at least we'll know exactly what we're dealing with, and then we can tender both options."

"Tender?" Dotty clarified.

"As in, getting builders to price them both."

"Are you thinking of opening up the whole of the first floor?" Marion asked brightly.

"It's an option. There's a lot of space up there," Zach replied.

"There certainly is. The only reason we haven't utilised it before is that it's been difficult to entice people up to it. But if they have a reason to go, and I presume you'll install a lift…"

"Yes, although that's another expense," Zach said, giving Dotty a faint smile.

"Are you concerned about the overall cost, or how you'll recover your investment, or Marmaduke's reaction?" Dotty asked.

"All three. And while Bernadette, Gilly, and I are moving forward, Marmaduke is still the company chairman until the board holds a special meeting to formally appoint me to the role and split off the estate agency business."

"What are we going to do about May's auction?" Dotty told him about Amanda selling her building to buy a country house to renovate.

"Is Cirencester Auctioneers closing?" Clara asked, her mouth falling open. "But after we've held this month's auction?"

"Oh yes, and we might be able to hold another one there before the sale process is completed, but I think we should plan to hold it here," Dotty said, meeting Zach's gaze.

"I understand. I'll see how we can work it into our proposals." He glanced at the remaining sandwich in Dotty's container.

She offered it to him.

Smiling his thanks, he said, "I need to check a couple of points the architect raised. See you all later." With a cheerful wave, he left the office.

"He seems far more energised these days," Marion observed. "He needs a purpose, and the building works are giving him that. I wouldn't like to be the one working out how to repair this place, or deal with Marmaduke," she added, flicking on the switch for the electric kettle at the back of the office.

"Nor me," thought Dotty, popping the final piece of her sandwich into her mouth.

CHAPTER THIRTY-FIVE

DOTTY

Dotty caught up with Marion and Clara while they settled at their desks in the rear office of Akemans auction house, sipping their cups of Darjeeling tea.

"And I'm expecting Dr Marston in …" she looked up at the wall clock, "ten minutes. Would you like to join the discussion?" she asked Clara.

"Oh, yes, please. I've done some more research this morning. I found the building in the photo. Deerfield House. It was near Leipzig and owned by Friedrich Albrecht, the wealthy man Dr Marston told us about, until it was destroyed after the end of the war."

"Well done, and that ties in nicely," Dotty said. "It links the Josef Stoitzner painting to the house, which we now know from the photograph that Pete visited, or perhaps even stayed at."

"It's rumoured the Nazis used it as a base, so there really could have been treasure stored there," Clara added excitedly.

"There was," confirmed Hugo Marston as he stepped into the office.

"We're not exactly sure how much, but I've found a record of some soldiers handing over items they recovered from a large house near Leipzig to the British military authorities. This was done under the system known as 'trophy registration', before the Russians took control of the area."

"Were they The Little Owls?" Dotty asked.

"That wasn't their official unit name, but here's a list of the soldiers. Do you recognise any of them?" He handed Dotty a printed sheet of paper.

She scanned the list, and her eyes fell immediately on the first name. Lieutenant Francis Tyndall. Further down, she spotted Corporal Pete Reynolds.

Clara turned the paper towards her and read out the remaining names. "Corporal Walter Jameson." She looked at Dotty, who nodded in recognition, then continued, "Private Albert Cooper and Private Robert Austin."

Dotty picked up the photograph of the soldiers in front of Deerfield House and read the note on the back. "Myself with the boys. Pete, Walt, Bert, Matt, Rob. Bert could be short for Albert, so the one missing from the printout is Matt," Dotty mused.

"Can I see that photo?" Hugo asked.

Dotty handed it over.

"And the others?"

Dotty gave him Pete's group photo and the one of Francis Tyndall on his own. Hugo glanced briefly at Francis's portrait before placing it back on her desk, but he held up the other two photos side by side.

"Do you recognise anyone in these?" Hugo asked, holding the photos out for Dotty and Clara to inspect.

"The officer is Francis Tyndall," Clara ventured.

"Yes, and the others?"

"No," Dotty and Clara both admitted, shaking their heads.

"What if I told you that the Matt mentioned on the back of this photo …" he raised the one with Deerfield House in the background, "is Sergeant Matthew Henshaw?"

"Really?" Dotty said, taking the photo from him. "The Matthew Henshaw we know is old enough to have fought in the war, but I don't recognise him in any of these young men."

"He's actually that one," Hugo said, pointing to a stocky man who Dotty realised appeared slightly older than the others.

"Oh," Dotty said, sounding deflated. "So he's not our Matthew Henshaw then."

"You mean the man who runs Athena Trading, don't you?" Clara asked. "He's thin, stooped, and, of course, old. But you know what? I bet he looked a bit like this when he was younger."

She pointed to the young man in Pete's photo, who wore a jumper with a hole in the sleeve rather than military uniform.

"But that's the unit's interpreter, a Czech called Anton Vašek," Hugo explained.

"Was he the one they named the unit after?" Dotty asked.

"Yes. They nicknamed him the Little Owl because of his ability to spot danger. Just a shame he couldn't save himself."

"Why?" Dotty asked. "What happened?"

"I found a report that he was travelling in an Austin Tilly when it was ambushed, and he was killed."

"Oh, that's really sad," Clara said softly. "He looks so young in the photograph."

"Would you like to know who made the report?" Hugo asked, his tone tinged with intrigue.

"Is it relevant?" Dotty responded.

"It could be," Hugo considered. "It was our elusive Sergeant Matthew Henshaw."

"He was elusive," Clara agreed. "He didn't attend The Little Owls reunion, although Bert's letter says an owl pendant was sent to him."

“Anyway,” Dotty said, handing the photograph back to Hugo, “This is all fascinating, but does it help us with the owl pendants or the painting?”

“The owl pendants, certainly. It’s clear that Francis Tyndall either deliberately kept a gold chalice from the treasure they found or stumbled upon it after handing everything else over. We’ll never know, but to avoid sullying Helen’s family name, let’s say it was the latter.

“He found the chalice and, wondering what best to do with it, asked Otto Mond to melt it down and create an owl pendant for each surviving member of his unit. He handed them out at the reunion in 1948. As you said, Matthew Henshaw didn’t attend, so Francis either sent or delivered his pendant to him.”

Clara tilted her head, considering Hugo’s words. “Does that mean we have to give Pete’s pendant back? Does it count as stolen Nazi treasure?”

“I wondered that myself,” Hugo remarked. “But no. We don’t have all the pendants, and they aren’t recognisable as part of the original chalice. Also, without any distinguishing marks, returning a gold chalice to its rightful owners would be nearly impossible."

Dotty nodded and smiled. "Beth will be happy to keep the pendant as a memory of Pete, and also of her great-grandfather if the police return the second one," Dotty said. "She seemed less enthusiastic about the painting, even though it's more valuable. Have you found out anything else about it?"

"As you were considering earlier, there's a definite link between the painting, Deerfield House, and Friedrich Albrecht, who owned both. Now, let's think about the situation The Little Owls found themselves in."

Dotty moved behind her desk and sat down. Marion brought a chair for Hugo, and then herself, while Clara collected her own. Once everyone was seated, Hugo began.

"It's 1946, the war has ended, and The Little Owls are relieved to be on the winning side. Their unit is tasked with creating an inventory of abandoned equipment. While working in Saxony, they find temporary shelter in Deerfield House, a partially ruined manor house. While there, they discover a stash of hidden treasure. Do you have that sketch Francis drew of it?"

Dotty opened the sketchbook on her desk and turned to the back page, rotating it so Hugo could see.

"Interesting," he said. "We have wrapped pictures, some furniture, and these boxes likely contain smaller, valuable items. So what does our group of intrepid soldiers do? They're deep in Soviet-controlled territory, and tensions between the Allies and Soviets are rising. Then they're ordered to return to England."

"Surely they pack up as much of the treasure as they can and bring it back," Clara reasoned.

"Yes, and I think that's exactly what they did. Now, back to our story," he continued, sitting up straighter. "Deerfield House held the treasure, but it also had some valuable items of its own. These would have fallen into Russian hands once The Little Owls left. So what do they do about them?"

"They took some of them too?" Clara suggested, caught up in the narrative.

"And that's how I think the soldiers came into possession of the Josef Stoitzner paintings."

"The gold chalice might also have been in the house," Dotty considered. "And the wooden box."

"What wooden box?" Hugo asked.

"One I found in Francis Tyndall's trunk," Dotty explained. "It's walnut, inlaid with mother-of-pearl. On the lid there's a tree of life surrounded by Hebrew writing."

"So the soldiers may have rescued valuable items from the house, along with the Nazi treasure. But what became of it all?" Hugo wondered aloud.

CHAPTER THIRTY-SIX

KEYA

After handing The Owl's Nook cafe back to Laura on Tuesday morning, Keya returned to her own Waterwheel Cafe.

She felt frustrated that she couldn't do more to help Lynn and Warren with their investigations into Helen Fletcher's death and the theft of the valuable comic annuals.

As she cleared away dirty plates and a half-eaten tuna sandwich, she thought about the difference between being a police officer actively investigating a case and her current role as a crime scene manager.

Her job felt more passive, confined to processing evidence at the scene rather than considering what might have happened.

It was a sharp contrast, and she found it frustrating. At least Lynn was keeping her involved. If only there was a way she could be more useful.

As she placed the dirty dishes on the counter, her phone vibrated in her pocket. Pulling it out, she felt a surge of anticipation when she recognised Warren's number.

"Hi. Do you have an update?" she asked, her tone eager.

"I do, and I wanted to ask you a question as I can't get hold of Inspector Lynn."

Keya unconsciously squared her shoulders. So she did still have a role to play.

"Of course, what is it?"

"I've been following up leads on the *Steel Sentinels* annuals and checking with traders to see if they've come across any of the missing ones."

"And someone has?"

"Yes. A shopkeeper in Gloucester bought a 1987 special edition hardback this morning."

"From Declan?"

"That's what I'm trying to figure out. The dealer asked for the seller's name and address for his records and was given 'Dan Cane' with an address in Farnham. When the dealer asked why he didn't sell it locally, the man said he was visiting relatives nearby."

"Did you visit the shopkeeper and show him Declan's photo?"

"No, I only spoke to him over the phone. I wanted to hear your thoughts before taking it any further."

Keya frowned. "It all sounds very suspicious. The shopkeeper was right to question why he didn't offer it to someone closer to home. It seems like he suspected something wasn't quite right. And Dan Cane. Declan Reid. It's not exactly a clever alias, but probably the best he could come up with at short notice."

"What do you think I should do next?" Warren asked.

"I'd hold off until you can speak to Lynn."

"What about a search warrant for Declan's room at the pub? Should I apply for one?"

"And say what? That you're looking for some comics? I doubt the Chief Inspector would sign off on that, let alone a judge. No, wait for Lynn. If I were her, I'd question Declan further, either about Helen's death, the break-in, or both. And if she visits Declan at his room in the pub, you could go with her and take a discreet look around. You'd need to be subtle, but most criminals aren't that clever. They often leave evidence lying around or in plain sight, especially if they don't think they need to hide it."

"OK, thanks. I'll discuss all this with Inspector Lynn."

"And you'll let me know how it goes?" Keya asked hopefully.

"Sure," Warren replied, and then rang off.

Keya returned to the routine activities of the cafe. An hour before closing time, she was surprised when Matthew Henshaw and his party entered.

"Good afternoon," she greeted them. "A table for

four?" She glanced back at Radek, Imogen, and Sebastian.

"Five," Matthew corrected. "Dr Marston will also be joining us."

Keya led them to a table by the window overlooking the waterwheel and took their drinks order.

As she returned with the drinks, Dr Marston arrived, his face flushed.

"You look excited," Matthew commented as Dr Marston pulled out a chair. He paused, and glanced around the group before he revealed, "I've uncovered a very exciting lead on some Second World War treasure."

"You have?" Matthew asked, just as Keya placed a pot of tea in front of him.

"Yes. Dotty Sayers, the manager of the auction house here, has been researching items she found during a routine house clearance. It turns out the house belonged to a soldier from a unit called The Little Owls."

Keya noted a sharp intake of breath but, looking

around the table, she couldn't pinpoint who it came from.

Matthew appeared politely interested, Imogen attentive, and Sebastian engrossed in his phone. Radek's expression remained unreadable as he sat stiffly in his chair.

"And how does this unit connect to wartime treasure?" Matthew pressed.

"Well…" Dr Marston began, then turned to Keya and asked, "Could I have a cappuccino?"

"Of course," Keya replied, leaving the table as Dr Marston launched into an explanation about a house in East Germany.

When she returned with Dr Marston's coffee, she heard him say, "…and by complete coincidence, the name of the soldier I still need to track down is Sergeant Matthew Henshaw."

Imogen laughed, teasing Matthew, "You haven't been hiding wartime treasure from us, have you, Grandad?"

Dr Marston smiled and added, "Your grandfather looks nothing like the photo we have of Sergeant Henshaw."

Again, Keya sensed a subtle shift in the atmosphere. But everyone at the table appeared relaxed, except for Radek, whose gaze darted anxiously around the room, a behaviour Keya had grown used to.

As she set Dr Marston's coffee down, Keya's mind drifted back to her earlier conversation with Lynn and Warren at The Owl's Nook. Although it wasn't strictly her role, she decided to ask, "Sebastian, can I ask what car you drive?"

Sebastian looked up, frowning. "Not that it's any of your business, but a red Tesla Model 3."

"Or my Mini," Imogen chimed in with a grin, "when he wants to be more discreet."

"And today we all came in my Range Rover," added Matthew. "Why do you ask?"

"We're trying to trace a car connected to a crime scene," Keya said simply.

"A crime scene? And you think Sebastian might be involved?" Imogen asked, laughing nervously.

Matthew turned toward Sebastian, his expression stern.

Again, aware that it wasn't really her place, but unwilling to let the opportunity slip by, Keya pressed on. "A witness saw Sebastian arrive at The Owl's Nook on the afternoon Helen Fletcher died."

"Explain yourself," Matthew growled at Sebastian, his tone sharp.

"I… um…" Sebastian stammered.

"Please don't tell me you were involved in Helen's death," Matthew demanded, banging his cane on the floor as he sat up straighter.

"No, I wasn't! I swear. She was alive when I left," Sebastian protested.

"Then what were you doing there?" Keya pressed.

"Yes, Sebastian," Matthew added, his voice cold. "What business did you have with Helen? You weren't trying to undermine your sister, were you?"

"As if," Imogen said with a dismissive chuckle.

Sebastian shot her a resentful glance but didn't respond immediately.

"I'm waiting," Matthew said, his voice low and steely. There was a faint trace of an accent that Keya couldn't quite place, but it was enough to silence those around the table.

Imogen stopped laughing and sipped her drink, while Sebastian shifted uncomfortably in his chair. Finally, he blurted out, "I was trying to persuade her to sell me the business."

"You? Run a bookshop?" Imogen exclaimed, her tone incredulous.

"Well, you told me it had loads of potential," Sebastian snapped. "And Declan said we could convert the building into flats."

"Declan Reid?" Keya asked sharply.

"Who is he?" Matthew interjected, his gaze narrowing.

"Laura Fletcher's ex-husband," Keya explained. "And why doesn't it surprise me that he was involved?"

"He's a blaggard," Radek said in his gravelly voice.

"When will you ever learn?" Matthew drawled, his tone heavy with disappointment. "If only you'd focus on the business we already have, who knows what you might achieve. But you always have to be scheming about something else."

"Something for me," Sebastian argued. "Athena Trading is your business, and Imogen has BrightEdge. What do I have?"

"All the opportunities in the world," Matthew replied curtly. "A successful business handed to you on a plate."

Imogen's gaze hardened. "While I had to make my own way, because the family business wasn't a place for a woman," she said, her voice tinged with sorrow and a trace of bitterness.

Matthew glanced at Radek, an unspoken exchange passing between them. Finally, he turned back to Imogen. "Perhaps that was a mistake. But if you'd come straight into the business, you wouldn't have found success for yourself." Though he spoke to Imogen, his gaze shifted to Sebastian.

Keya cleared her throat, breaking the tension. "Sebastian, would you mind making a formal statement to one of my colleagues? To explain what you were doing at The Owl's Nook that Saturday afternoon, and what time you arrived. By the way, when did you leave? And did you see anyone else?"

Sebastian hesitated. "I left sometime between half past three and four o'clock. I don't know exactly. But as I drove away, I saw four people on bikes turning into the car park."

The cyclists Warren had mentioned, Keya thought. Who arrived just before four.

"We've interviewed some cyclists, and the time frames fit," Keya confirmed.

Sebastian looked visibly relieved.

"So, is he off the hook?" Imogen asked, a hint of disappointment in her voice.

Sebastian shot her a confused look, but she just smiled playfully back at him.

"For the time being," Keya replied. "Unless any other evidence surfaces. But I warn you," she added, fixing her gaze on Sebastian, "be open, frank, and honest with my colleague. If you hide anything, we'll find out, and it won't look good for you."

"I agree," Matthew said, his voice heavy with finality. "Secrets have a way of coming to light, sooner or later."

CHAPTER THIRTY-SEVEN

KEYA

On Wednesday morning, Keya visited the wife of a dairy farmer who'd started producing a new range of organic yoghurts. She liked them but wasn't sure how to incorporate them into the cafe's menu.

Returning to Akemans, she parked her car and strode towards the large oak doors at the entrance to the antique centre.

"Morning!" Dotty called as she stepped out of the auction house.

They walked towards each other, and Keya asked, "Where are you off to? Visiting a new client?" She noticed that Dotty was wearing her blue padded jacket and carrying a tote bag with a manila folder poking out from the top.

"I wish. No, Hugo—Dr Marston—just called. Apparently, Matthew Henshaw has some information about the treasure he's been trying to trace from the Second World War, and possibly about the painting and owl pendants."

"That's interesting," Keya said. "I heard them discussing that yesterday, and Matthew didn't seem to know anything about it."

She paused, reflecting on the subtle shift in atmosphere during that conversation.

"Or maybe he just didn't want to say anything in front of his grandchildren."

"Well, I'll soon find out. He's sending a car to collect me."

Keya felt her phone vibrate and she said, "Good luck" to Dotty before answering the call.

It was the dairy farmer's wife. Already? She sighed quietly before responding. "Hi."

The woman launched into a cheerful monologue

about how lovely it had been to meet Keya and how wonderful it would be to work together.

Keya listened patiently, waiting for an opportunity to interrupt. When she finally could, she said, “Of course, but as I mentioned, we need to see if there’s a way to incorporate the yoghurts into our menu.”

Undeterred, the farmer’s wife continued her lengthy sales pitch. Keya, growing frustrated but trying to remain polite, glanced towards the car park.

Dotty waved and climbed into a sporty silver Mercedes.

Keya waved back distractedly, then froze. A sporty silver Mercedes.

With a scattering of gravel, the car accelerated out of the car park.

Keya ran to catch a better look as the car slowed. Then it pulled out onto the road, heading towards the village of Coln Akeman, but just as it turned, she caught sight of the last two letters on its number plate. P and Q.

Lifting her phone back to her ear, she realised the farmer's wife was still talking. "Hello? Are you there, Keya?"

"Sorry, I have to go. I'll be in touch," she said hurriedly, before ending the call. She immediately searched for Warren's number and dialled it.

"Morning," Warren answered cheerfully. "Inspector Lynn and I are just returning to the station with Declan Reid. You were right. We found some of the *Steel Sentinels* annuals in his room at the pub."

"Great, but listen," Keya said, her voice rising with urgency. "There's a problem."

"What's wrong?" Warren asked, his tone sharpening.

"It's Dotty. I just saw her drive off in a sporty silver Mercedes."

There was a slight pause before Lynn's voice came on the line. "Do you think it's the same one the cyclists saw at The Owl's Nook?"

"That's what I'm worried about," Keya replied. "I spoke to Dotty just before she left. She said she was going to see Matthew Henshaw. Dr Marston had called her to arrange the meeting."

"Then we need to check if either of them owns a car like that. Can you tell me anything more about it?" Lynn asked.

"I tried to get the number plate, but I only caught the last two letters which were P and Q."

"Got it. Leave it with me," Lynn said, her tone firm. "I'll look into it. And don't worry, I'm sure Dotty will be fine."

Keya ended the call but felt far from reassured. Dotty had been digging into long-buried secrets which someone might not want to be exposed.

But Dr Hugo Marston? Keya frowned. He'd seemed genuinely excited yesterday about uncovering new information on wartime treasure. Dotty had mentioned his role was to find and return such items to their rightful owners.

Surely, he wouldn't hurt Helen, or Dotty, unless they'd discovered he was doing something illegal. Could he be selling off some of the treasure or making deals to keep certain pieces hidden?

It didn't sit right with her. The few times she'd met Dr Marston he'd come across as open and honest. And yesterday, there'd been a childlike enthusiasm in the way he'd described the new lead. But criminals could be charming. She'd met enough of them to know that.

Matthew Henshaw was certainly charming. But he'd built his business from nothing, and few people achieved that by playing fair. What had he said the previous afternoon about secrets having a way of coming to light?

Could Dotty have uncovered something he wanted to stay hidden? And could he have arranged for her to be taken to stop her revealing it?

Keya's pulse quickened. Was Dotty in real danger while she stood in Akemans' car park doing nothing to help?

Her phone rang, jolting her out of her thoughts. She answered it quickly. "Lynn?"

"We've checked. Neither Dr Marston nor Matthew Henshaw has a Mercedes registered to them," Lynn informed her. "I'm almost back at the station, and I've asked one of the constables to run a check on the partial number plate. I'll update you as soon as I hear anything."

Lynn hung up, leaving Keya staring towards the road to Coln Akeman.

She couldn't just stand here. But what could she do to help Dotty?

Her grip tightened on her phone. She had to tell Zach. Maybe he'd know what to do.

CHAPTER THIRTY-EIGHT

DOTTY

Dotty climbed into the smart little silver car beside Hugo and said, "This is nice. But I was surprised to receive your call."

"Not as surprised as I was to receive Matthew's message," replied Hugo.

"Do you know what it's about?"

Hugo glanced at Radek in the driver's seat as he accelerated out of Akemans' car park. "No, I'm afraid not. Although I did tell Matthew about The Little Owls, the treasure, and the other Matthew Henshaw yesterday, after I left you."

"Perhaps he's a relative, and Matthew has information about him."

"That would be very useful, as I'm still waiting for a contact at the MOD to get back to me, and that could take several days."

They chatted amiably for a few minutes, but Dotty's grip on her white tote bag tightened as a faint unease began to creep in. She asked, "Do you know where we're going?"

"I don't, actually. I received a message from Matthew's company email address saying a car would collect me at half past nine from the guest house where I stay when I'm down here. It also asked me to contact you and arrange to pick you up afterwards. And here we are. But I have no idea where we're going. My last few meetings with Matthew have all been at the Waterwheel Cafe."

Dotty leaned forward, glancing at Radek. "Could you tell us where we're heading?"

"It's not too far," Radek replied curtly, keeping his eyes fixed on the road ahead.

Dotty pursed her lips. She didn't like evasive answers, and she was still uneasy about Radek after seeing his hostile reaction to the salesman in the cafe.

Pulling her phone out of her bag, she quickly messaged Zach.

I'm with Hugo on my way to meet Matthew Henshaw. Not sure exactly where we're going, or when I'll be back.

The reply came almost immediately:

Where are you going? Who is driving?

Why was Zach asking about the driver?

Not sure where we are going. Radek is driving.

"Is everything OK?" Hugo asked.

"Oh, yes," Dotty replied, although a note of uncertainty crept into her voice. Zach's questions had only added to her anxiety. "Zach, who you met at the talk, is putting together plans to upgrade the auction house, and he wants to meet me to discuss them."

Which was partly true, she told herself, although

she wasn't entirely sure why she felt the need to tell a small lie.

"What is he proposing?" Hugo asked conversationally.

Hugo seemed perfectly relaxed, so why was her stomach churning?

Her phone buzzed with another message:

Tap on the Find My Phone app I installed for you and share your location with me. Just add my phone number.

Why did he want her to do that? Still, at least he'd know where she was if something did happen.

But nothing was going to happen, she told herself firmly, and she hesitated for a moment before deciding she would follow Zach's instructions.

"Sorry, I just need to do something," Dotty told Hugo distractedly as she fumbled with the app. After a few taps, she managed to share her location with Zach.

"That should do it," she murmured, slipping her phone back into her bag.

"This isn't Athena's offices, or Matthew's house," Hugo said sharply, leaning forward and addressing Radek.

Dotty looked up as they turned between a pair of crumbling stone gateposts, their weathered surfaces thick with moss and ivy.

Radek said nothing from the front.

"I say, where are we?" Hugo's voice carried a sharp edge of indignation.

"Nearly there," Radek said flatly.

"Yes, but where?" Hugo pressed.

Radek remained silent as the car bumped down a neglected drive. He slowed to manoeuvre around deep potholes as the tyres crunched over broken tarmac.

They emerged in front of a large house. It must once have been grand, but now its former splendour was long faded. The windows were grimy and cracked, the facade weathered and scarred, and the stonework was pockmarked and crumbling.In a voice filled with concern and confusion, Dotty repeated, "Yes, where are we?"

CHAPTER THIRTY-NINE

KEYA

Keya finally stopped staring at the road where Dotty had driven away in the silver Mercedes and quickly called Zach.

"Hi, Keya," he answered brightly.

"Where are you?"

"In Gilly's office. She lets me use it when I'm at Akemans."

"Stay there. I'm coming."

"Keya…" Zach exclaimed, his tone uneasy, but she didn't stop to explain. Pocketing her phone, she jogged back to the antique centre. Inside, she ignored the curious stares as she rushed past and took the metal staircase two steps at a time.

Zach was waiting for her at the top.

"Are you okay?" he asked as she reached the first floor, slightly breathless.

"I'm fine, but I'm worried about Dotty. Did she tell you where she was going this morning?"

"I wasn't aware she was going anywhere. She told me she'd be working here all day."

"Well, I've just seen her climb into the same make of car we've been trying to trace from the crime scene at The Owl's Nook. She said Hugo Marston called her and that she was going to join him for a meeting with Matthew Henshaw."

"I know she's been working closely with Dr Marston, and he's also collaborating on a charity project with Matthew Henshaw. But tell me more about the car."

Keya did.

"I'm sure that type of car's pretty common," Zach said, frowning. "But it's strange that neither Hugo nor Matthew drives one."

A ping interrupted them. Zach pulled out his phone and glanced at the screen.

"It's a message from Dotty," he said.

Keya held her breath as Zach read it aloud.

"I'm with Hugo on my way to meet Matthew Henshaw. Not sure exactly where we're going, or when I'll be back."

"On her way to meet?" Keya repeated, her brow furrowing. "So Matthew's not with them." Her mind raced. "Ask her who's driving."

Zach quickly tapped out a reply, and the response came back just as fast.

"She says she doesn't know where they're going, but Radek is driving."

"That makes sense since he does drive for Matthew," Keya admitted, although her stomach still twisted with unease. "But why that car?"

"I'll ask her to turn on the 'Find My Phone' app I installed," Zach said, already typing the request.

While he did, Keya called Lynn.

"Any news from Dotty?" Lynn asked immediately.

"She says Radek is driving. Do we know if he owns a silver Mercedes?"

"Just a moment."

Keya switched her phone to speaker mode and heard muffled voices in the background before Lynn returned.

This time, her tone was serious. "Radek does own a silver Mercedes with the registration number WX21 APQ."

"That must be the one Dotty's in," Keya said grimly.

"But why would Radek—or his car—have been at The Owl's Nook?" Lynn wondered aloud.

"Never mind that," Keya said, her voice firm. "If there's even the faintest chance Radek was involved in Helen's death, protecting Dotty needs to be our priority."

"And Dr Marston? You said they're together?"

"I didn't see him. All I know is that he called

Dotty about the meeting. Maybe he and Radek are in this together."

"But why would he be? Does he know Radek that well? And why would he want to harm Helen, or Dotty?" asked Lynn sounding perplexed.

"Because maybe they discovered he was doing something shady," Keya speculated. "Like selling the very treasures he's supposed to be returning to families."

"I suppose anything's possible at this point," Lynn mused. "Do we have any idea where Dotty is heading?"

Keya glanced at Zach and asked him, "Can you see where she is?"

Zach nodded, showing her the app.

Keya focused on the scene as she relayed the information to Lynn. "She's travelling along a minor road heading west from Northleach."

"Northleach?" Lynn repeated on speakerphone. "They could be travelling to see Matthew Henshaw. His office is in Cheltenham and he lives just outside Naunton."

"But what if she's not?" Zach asked, his calm demeanour giving way to genuine concern.

"I'm not sure, but I don't like that she's in that car. I'm not one to overreact," Lynn said firmly, "and I can't issue an alert to all units. But I think that Warren and I should head in that direction now. Declan Reid will just have to wait in the cells for another hour or so."

"Declan Reid?" Zach asked, confused.

"Never mind," Lynn replied. "Keep me updated on Dotty's location."

"Will do," Keya promised, ending the call.

As she did, Zach turned to her. "We're not just going to wait here for Lynn to find Dotty, are we?"

"No, of course not. You'd better drive in case we need to go off-road."

Zach nodded, his expression serious. "And you can track Dotty and keep Lynn updated. Let's go."

CHAPTER FORTY

DOTTY

"Welcome to Deerpark House," Radek said as he opened Dotty's car door, his tone clipped but polite.

"Deerpark?" she repeated, her brow furrowing. Surely it couldn't be a coincidence that this house had the same name as the wartime one she thought as she climbed out of the car.

She and Hugo exchanged a quick glance before following Radek. He strode ahead purposefully, leading them past the front of the house and around to the side, where a crumbling wall jutted awkwardly from the structure.

Radek stepped round the wall and looked up at the black windows. Glass was missing, and the frames were disintegrating with rot.

"Matthew bought this fifteen years ago, intending to renovate it and give the house new life. But as the years passed, his energy and focus shifted. So here it stands, slowly falling into wrack and ruin, forgotten, just like its namesake. That is, until you two," Radek snapped, making Dotty flinch, "started asking questions about the original one."

Her stomach knotted at his sharp tone, but her curiosity was piqued as she asked, "Do you mean the one in East Germany?"

"The one I thought was buried when the Russians destroyed it," Radek said curtly. "Matthew said secrets have a habit of coming to light, but I disagree. Some can remain buried. It just requires action to keep them that way."

"I don't follow," said Hugo. "What secrets are we talking about? And where is Matthew? I thought we were meeting him."

"This centres around The Little Owls, doesn't it?" Dotty ventured. "And the painting and pendant I discovered at Pete Reynolds' house, after he died…" Her voice trailed off.

Pete had died after falling down stairs at a veterans' charity event.

Fallen, or pushed?

No, surely that was too far-fetched.

Puzzled, she looked at Radek and said, "You're too young to have had anything to do with that wartime unit. But you're Czech, aren't you? Was the interpreter a relative?"

It was the only connection she could make in what felt like a bizarre, almost comical situation. She half expected Radek to pull out a gun and force them into the house or around the back to where there was a large hole, like something out of a film.

She jumped as Radek exclaimed, "*Ich bin kein Tscheche*!"

Dotty stared at him. She'd never seen him lose his cool before. And had he just spoken in German?

"You're not Czech?" Hugo said, his voice puzzled. "Are you German?"

Radek didn't reply immediately. Instead, he closed his eyes briefly and took a steadying breath, his hands clenching into fists. When he spoke, his voice was measured but carried a sharp edge. "I am German. And I have nothing to do with a Czech interpreter or The Little Owls."

"You said 9th November 1989 changed everything," Dotty remembered.

"That's right," Hugo agreed, "and I wondered why Matthew gave you that strange look. Of course, he expected you to say the 17th of November. That's when Czechoslovakia's Velvet Revolution began. The 9th was when the Berlin Wall fell."

Hugo squinted as he stared at Radek, and his body tensed. Then, in a voice full of disapproval, he demanded, "Does Matthew know what you are?"

"What he is?" Dotty asked, confused. "I don't understand."

Despite the potentially dangerous situation they found themselves in, when Hugo spoke he sounded as though he were giving one of his talks.

He turned to Dotty and revealed, “When the wall came down, the people who actually had to fight for their freedom, or find ways to cover their true identity, were those within the regime who had persecuted the people of East Germany. And the worst amongst them were the Stasi.”

A muscle twitched in Radek’s cheek.

“The secret police? But surely you were too young,” she said, addressing Radek directly.

He snorted. “You were never too young for them. They started with us at school. We had little choice. Join, or face a life in the factories like our parents. Enlist, and you could move to Berlin, have your own flat, a future. A better life.”

“So you joined them?”

“What would you have done?” His voice grew sharper. “And I wasn’t alone. We were a group of three friends. Their summer camps were hard, with long days and tough discipline. But we were well fed, allowed to watch banned American films, and taught that the West was full of degenerates and liars.”

“I think that’s called brainwashing,” Hugo said dryly.

Radek laughed bitterly. “Call it what you like. We were children. They made sure we believed it.”

Dotty might have felt some sympathy if the discussion were happening somewhere else. But in front of a derelict house? What intentions did Radek have? And where was Matthew?

Hugo ventured, “So when the wall fell, you saw your opportunity for freedom?”

Radek narrowed his eyes. “Freedom?” He laughed, and it was an unpleasant sound. “Survival. I knew everything would change. And it did. People like me, collaborators and part of the regime, we had targets on our backs. Everyone was out for revenge or retribution, so I wasn’t about to hang around.”

“So you ran?” Hugo made it sound more like a statement than a question.

“Of course I ran. I was twenty-two. Everything I’d known collapsed overnight. At first, I didn’t even know where to go, but when Czechoslovakia followed East Germany, I saw my chance. I could blend in there, disappear. I reinvented myself, changed my name, became Czech. It wasn't about freedom. It was about staying alive."

"But you didn't stay in Czechoslovakia?" questioned Dotty.

"No, why would I? I worked my way across Europe, kept a low profile, and joined a group of Czech labourers. In 1994 we were recruited for construction work in London, and I moved to England."

It all made sense, and Dotty thought it sounded plausible.

And Radek's tone was calm, and his manner composed.

"How did you meet Matthew?" she asked, trying to link the past with the present.

"At a Czech social club he sometimes visited and supported."

"But why would he do that?" Dotty wondered if it had been one of the charities or organisations he'd donated to.

"Surely you don't need to ask. Or haven't you put that part of the puzzle together yet?" Radek said, staring at Dotty.

Dotty had to admit that she was at a loss.

Radek turned to Hugo. "You said you were waiting for someone from the military to get in touch. Then you'll figure it out. Pete Reynolds understood. He recognised Matthew. Not immediately, but when he did, he pieced everything together."

"Sorry, I'm lost," Hugo said, scratching his head. "What does Pete Reynolds have to do with this?"

"If Pete recognised Matthew, then this does lead back to The Little Owls." As Dotty had initially thought. "And Matthew was involved, but I still don't see him as the man in the photograph."

Then Dotty remembered Clara's observation. She felt her jaw tighten as she realised what it meant, but even though she forced herself to relax, Radek's lips curved into a nasty, malicious grin.

"He wasn't the soldier, was he? Matthew was the interpreter." Dotty's voice was barely above a whisper.

Hugo turned to her, his lips parted in confusion. Then he asked, "The one they called The Little Owl?"

Whack. Dotty screamed.

CHAPTER FORTY-ONE

DOTTY

She hadn't meant to cry out, but Radek had moved so swiftly.

He acted with the agility of a man half his age. Perhaps he'd already planned his move, but picking up the stone and striking Hugo over the head had happened in a blur.

"And you'll be next," Radek warned, his voice low and menacing. His unflinching glare and cold precision revealed the dangerous man he must once have been—and clearly still was.

Dotty instinctively stepped back, her heart pounding.

"Everything we've built, Matthew and I."

"Is this about money? About Matthew donating to charities?" Dotty couldn't help asking, even though it didn't seem to fit. Why would that bother Radek?

"I don't care if he gives it all away. It would serve that self-centred parasite Sebastian right," Radek spat.

Dotty noticed that he didn't mention Imogen, but this wasn't the time for such observations. Not with Hugo collapsed on the rubble-littered ground, moaning as blood seeped from his head.

Radek's eyes blazed with unhinged fury.

"If it's not the money, then what?" Dotty pressed, even though her intuition screamed at her to stop pushing Radek.

She stepped sideways, keeping her movements slow and deliberate, trying to put some distance between herself and Radek. She wanted to draw his attention away from Hugo, so he wouldn't be tempted to strike him again.

But all the while, she kept her gaze on Radek.

Radek's eyes followed her, unyielding. "The truth," he hissed. "If people knew who Matthew really was, who I really am, everything we've built would collapse. It's not about the money, but about what we've created. A new life. A better life. Leaving the past behind, starting over. Reinvention comes at a cost, and now you want to destroy it all with your questions and meddling."

His voice grew sharper, a sneer twisting his face. "Matthew deserves better than to have it all fall apart because of you two. Because of that soldier, and the daughter."

"Do you mean Francis Tyndall? And Helen? Did you kill her?" Dotty asked, her voice tight.

"I silenced her. She was also threatening our past," Radek spat. "The truth about who we were and where we came from. She was going to unearth things that should remain hidden. If she had exposed us, everything we've worked so hard to protect would have been ruined. Matthew's life, my life. Do you think people like you wouldn't condemn us for what we've done?"

"But how was she threatening you?" Dotty asked, still confused.

"She started asking questions about her father. After all this time. Why now? Then she turned to Peter Reynolds, and he became suspicious. And when he met Matthew…"

"He recognised him as The Little Owl, the unit's interpreter," Dotty said, as she once again remembered Clara's comment about the old photos and Matthew's resemblance to the interpreter.

Despite the precariousness of her situation, Dotty pressed on, determined to uncover the truth. "Did you push Pete?"

"He was an old man. It was easy. I'm not proud of it. But I couldn't have him reveal Matthew's secret. His past. What he'd done."

"You were protecting Matthew?"

"Of course. That's my job. My role. Matthew's name is everything. I couldn't risk ruining his reputation. I had to act. I was right to act."

Dotty wondered what kind of secret could drive a man to kill not once, but twice, and now possibly again. Something in Matthew's past? Something Radek believed had to remain buried at all costs.

She refused to let her thoughts spiral. She had to keep him talking.

From the hard, unblinking look in his eyes, there was no doubt about his intentions for her or for Hugo.

Hugo. He was still moaning on the ground, blood trickling into the dust. Dotty took another cautious step sideways, edging further from him. Radek followed, his eyes locked on hers.

Trying to buy herself and Hugo time, she asked, "What's your real name?"

Radek blinked, momentarily caught off guard. In a quiet, almost confused voice, he replied, "Jürgen Braun."

"That's nice." Dotty forced herself to smile, attempting to defuse the situation. She watched as fleeting emotions flickered across Radek's usually controlled face. Was he thinking back to happier, simpler times?

"Braun was my father's name, and Jürgen came from my mother." His voice softened briefly. "I never found out what happened to either of them."

"I'm sorry. That must have been hard, not knowing what became of them," Dotty said gently.

"Yes." His tone sharpened, and he stepped closer, his narrowed eyes boring into hers. "But I left them behind when I left Jürgen Braun behind."

Dotty realised he'd had enough of talking. Her breath quickened as she took another step back.

Radek's face shifted, becoming cold and unreadable, like a mask. She knew instinctively she wouldn't be able to reach him again.

He glanced briefly at Hugo, still crumpled on the ground, and then turned his now hard, cold gaze back to her. Without breaking eye contact, he bent down and picked up another stone. There were so many scattered around this collapsed section of the house.

Dotty's stomach lurched as he straightened, testing the stone's weight in his hand. His grip tightened, and all she wanted to do was flee.

Radek's voice was icy and barely above a whisper as he uttered, "I've kept us safe for decades." He stepped forward, slowly and deliberately. "I won't let you destroy everything we've built."

Dotty stumbled backwards, her shoulder slamming against the rough stone wall of the house. The cold, jagged surface dug into her back, grounding her as her panic rose. "Radek, you don't have to …" she started, her voice trembling, but he kept advancing.

His movements were unrelenting. She pressed her palms against the wall, the sharp edges biting into her skin as she tried to edge sideways.

Radek tilted his head, his unblinking eyes narrowing further, tracking her every move. "Stay still," he hissed softly.

But Dotty couldn't. She ducked suddenly, throwing herself to the side. Her feet slipped on loose stones, and she staggered, but she was desperate to create distance between herself and the man who'd clearly made up his mind to kill her.

Her foot caught. Stuck. And she was falling. She reached out, but her hands slid on the loose gravel. And then footsteps. And a shadow loomed over her.

CHAPTER FORTY-TWO

KEYA

"Can't you drive any faster?" Keya urged, holding a phone in each hand.

"Not on these roads," Zach protested as he braked hard to avoid a lone cyclist and negotiated a sharp left-hand bend. "How much further?"

Glancing at Zach's phone she replied, "Seven minutes to where Dotty's dot has stopped."

In her other hand, her phone rang.

"Whoa!" exclaimed Warren on the other end of the line.

"Sorry," Keya heard Lynn call out in the background. "I nearly missed the turn."

"Has Dotty's location changed?" Warren asked urgently.

"No," Keya replied, checking Zach's phone again. "And we're about six minutes away."

"We're ten," said Warren. "So you should get there first."

"Tell them to wait for us!" Lynn's voice called out.

"Did you hear that?" Warren asked.

"I did, but I hope Lynn doesn't expect Zach or me to take any notice. We won't be hanging around while Dotty is in danger."

"Just be careful," Warren warned. "Lynn spoke to Matthew Henshaw, and while he was very cagey, he did warn us that Radek is a dangerous man if provoked. When this is over, she's going to get to the bottom of …"

"We all are," Keya interjected. "But for now, we need to make sure Dotty is safe."

"And Dr Marston," Warren added quickly. "Whoa. I better go."

"Any change?" Zach asked, his voice serious as Keya ended the call.

Keya checked the other phone again. "No, at least her phone is in the same place. I just hope that means she is too."

They crossed the A40 and turned onto a narrow lane, little more than a rough track. Zach weaved from side to side, steering around the potholes that pitted its edges. Trees arched overhead, their shadows dappling the surface in the weak sunlight.

Keya would have found the new spring growth on the trees and hedgerows invigorating, were she not so worried about her friend.

Why, oh why, had she let Dotty climb into that car?

"Don't beat yourself up," Zach said, glancing at her. "You couldn't have known she was getting into a car with a mad man."

"I'm not sure he is mad," Keya replied grimly. "Just dangerous. If he killed Helen, then …"

"Stop!" Zach interrupted, braking hard.

A rabbit darted across the road, completely oblivious to the danger it was in.

Keya dropped the phones as she instinctively slapped her hands against the dashboard and braced herself. She exhaled a long, shaky breath as Zach accelerated forward.

Picking up Zach's phone, she stared at the screen and said, "We're nearly there. The turning should be in another two hundred metres, on the left." Then, spotting something in the distance, she added, "Look! There are some stone pillars up ahead."

Zach slowed as they approached the turn, manoeuvring the Jeep between the crumbling stone columns.

The track was barely drivable, its broken tarmac jarring them at every bump. They emerged from round a bend, and Keya caught her breath as the derelict country house came into view.

"What a fantastic view it must have had," she murmured, briefly distracted by the panorama of rolling Cotswold hills.

But her focus quickly sharpened as she spotted the silver Mercedes parked up ahead.

"That's the car," she said urgently as Zach braked to a stop beside it.

"I think it's empty," Zach replied, already opening his door before turning off the engine. In two quick strides, he reached the Mercedes and yanked open the back door.

Then he straightened up, holding Dotty's tote bag aloft.

Hurrying round the side of the Jeep, Keya called, "Is her phone in there?"

Zach turned back to the Mercedes and hastily emptied the bag's contents onto the back seat.

"Yes," he said, his voice tense. "But there's no sign of her."

A piercing scream shattered the silence.

Zach jerked his head towards the sound. "That was Dotty."

"But where did it come from?" Keya asked, her pulse quickening as she scanned the area.

"The side of the house," Zach replied, abandoning Dotty's bag and moving swiftly away.

"Zach!" Keya called after him.

"What?" He paused momentarily.

"Nothing." Keya ran to catch up with him. Despite Lynn's instructions, she'd told Warren they wouldn't wait if they thought Dotty was in danger.

The front door hung at a drunken angle on its hinges. It didn't look like anyone had passed that way.

Zach seemed confident about where he was heading as he picked his way round a rusting yellow cement mixer and piles of stones and sand. Keya scrambled after him, her heart pounding.

A male voice rumbled nearby, but she couldn't make out the words. Was it Radek?

Then she heard a softer, higher-pitched voice. Dotty. She was still alive. Relief flooded through her, and her pace quickened.

As Keya reached a crumbling archway, Zach held out his arm and pressed a finger to his lips.

They listened and heard Radek say clearly, "Matthew deserves better than to have it all destroyed because of you two. Because of that soldier, and the daughter."

Keya glanced at Zach, her eyes questioning.

He shrugged slightly and looked ahead.

Once, there must have been another room attached to the side of the house as there was a broken section of wall and the ground was littered with broken bricks, stones, pieces of wood, and sheets of corrugated metal.

How could they approach the voices silently and stealthily?

Zach scanned the ground, clearly thinking the same thing as he searched for a path through the debris.

"I silenced her. She was also threatening our past," she heard Radek growl.

She presumed Zach had also heard the words and the menace behind them as he stepped carefully forward.

Keya followed in his footsteps. Now she could hear Dotty's confused voice.

"But how was she threatening you?" Dotty didn't sound hurt or too afraid.

Keya realised her hands were shaking.

But what about Dr Marston? She hadn't heard him speak yet. As they picked their way towards the partially standing side wall, she thought she heard another vehicle. Was it Lynn and Warren? She dared not look round as she concentrated on the uneven ground.

The next thing she heard was Dotty ask, "Did you push Pete?"

Was Dotty referring to her deceased client, whose house she'd found the other pendant in?

Zach looked back at her, his forehead wrinkled with uncertainty.

She heard the car again, closer this time. Both she and Zach turned to watch a blue and yellow checked police car brake to a halt beside Zach's Jeep. She was relieved they hadn't announced their presence with flashing lights and a siren.

Since Dotty didn't appear to be in immediate danger, should they wait for Lynn and Warren?

Then the next question she heard Dotty ask caught her by surprise. "What's your real name?"

Why did Dotty think Radek had another name?

"Jürgen Braun," she heard Radek reply almost conversationally. That sounded German.

Keya turned around to watch Lynn and Warren as she heard Radek explain the origin of his former name. She waved, and Lynn opened her arms in a questioning gesture.

Keya pointed to the wall in front of Zach.

A change in Radek's tone immediately drew her attention back to his and Dotty's conversation.

Zach shifted his stance as if he were preparing to spring.

They heard the crunch of stone and the movement of gravel. Either Dotty, or Radek, or both were moving.

Keya tensed. She felt the atmosphere change.

Someone stumbled, and then Dotty's panicked voice cried, "Radek, you don't have to …"

Zach sprang forward, jumping over the lower end of the broken wall.

Keya followed, scrambling over stone debris.

"Stay still," muttered Radek, his back to Zach.

Dotty stopped edging along the wall. She stared at Radek and then, suddenly, she ducked and threw herself away from the building.

But her feet slipped on the loose rocks.

Keya remained focused on Dotty, although she was aware of Zach advancing quickly ahead of her. Dotty shifted again, but her foot caught in a hole. She tugged at it, but it was stuck.

Keya rushed towards Dotty as Zach hurled himself at Radek. Was he holding a rock?

No time to think.

She reached for Dotty, but it was too late. Her friend tumbled to the ground, her hands slipping on the loose rocks. Keya bent over her and, in a breathless voice, gasped, "Are you OK?"

CHAPTER FORTY-THREE

DOTTY

"Hugo, he's hurt," Dotty murmured, her voice tight with worry.

"I've got Radek," Lynn called across, her tone steady. "Warren, the handcuffs."

Dotty then heard a sharp metallic click, followed by the faint scrape of metal against metal. A snarling exhale followed, like an animal backed into a corner.

"Radek Novák, I am arresting you on suspicion of assault and attempted grievous bodily harm." Warren's voice was firm, filled with authority and pride as he recited the caution, "You have the right to remain silent…"

"Stay still," Keya whispered kindly to Dotty.

"I'd rather get up," Dotty replied, "but my foot's stuck."

She felt Keya gently wriggle her foot, loosening it bit by bit until, finally, she was able to lift it free.

"How is she?" Zach asked, squatting beside Keya.

"She has a name, and I'm fine, if someone could now help me up," Dotty said, feeling both sore and a little foolish.

Zach helped her stand, but as soon as she put weight on her left foot, it buckled. His grip tightened, steadying her.

"We'll need to get someone to look at that, and there's blood on your jeans," Keya noted, her tone professional.

"I've called an ambulance," Lynn said, crouching beside Hugo. Dotty realised that she'd placed her coat under his head for support.

"Do you have a blanket or another coat I could use to cover Dr Marston?" Lynn asked, looking over at Dotty, Keya, and Zach.

Radek was being led away by Warren. His arms were pinned behind his back so he couldn't attack anyone else, and the handcuffs glinted in the sunlight.

"Let me check the back of my Jeep," Zach said, but then he hesitated, glancing at Dotty, who was still leaning on him.

"I'll go," Keya volunteered, carefully picking her way across the uneven ground towards the front of the derelict house.

"You should sit," Zach said, glancing around.

There wasn't anywhere obvious Dotty could perch.

"Back at my car," Zach suggested.

"Just a minute," Lynn called. "I'm not going to ask for all the details now, but just tell me this, do you think anyone else is in danger?"

Dotty shook her head. "They might have been if you hadn't stopped Radek."

"You stopped him. Or at least Zach did when he flung himself at him. Have you ever played rugby?" Lynn asked Zach.

"No, nor was I really interested in American football, but I wasn't going to let him strike Dotty with that rock."

"Well, it was brave of you. Do we know which rock it was?" They all looked down at the many stones scattered across the ground.

"I'm not having every single one tested for his fingerprints," Keya declared, returning with a tartan picnic blanket.

"Nor would I ask you to. Besides, I think Warren captured Zach's moment of heroism on his phone," said Lynn with a grin as she took the blanket from Keya. Unfurling it, she placed the softer side over Hugo and added, "That should be enough to convict Radek."

"Is Hugo all right?" Dotty asked. "He hasn't said anything."

"I'm certain he has a concussion, but he is conscious. I told him he had to lie still and keep quiet, and at least he listens to my orders."

Zach actually blushed, and Keya looked up at the blue sky.

"Ow," Dotty moaned. She couldn't pinpoint the pain, but the numbness in her hands and knees was fading, leaving them feeling sore and raw.

"Come on, let's get you to my car. Keya, can you help?" Zach asked.

Dotty felt useless and burdensome as Zach and Keya linked hands to create a seat and carried her across the rough, debris-covered ground. Once in front of the house, she managed to hobble the short distance to the Jeep with Zach's help.

"In you go. Mind your head," Warren said to Radek as he assisted him into the back of the police car.

Radek didn't utter a sound.

"Ow," Dotty muttered again, as she settled on the back seat of Zach's Jeep. She wished she could be braver.

"I'm not sure what I can do to help," Zach said, his voice full of genuine concern.

"It sounds like you've done enough. Did you really rugby tackle Radek?"

"No, I …"

"Yes, look at this," Warren interrupted, hurrying towards the Jeep.

Dotty took his phone. "Oh dear, that wasn't a very ladylike fall," she remarked, watching herself waver before crumpling to the ground.

But the camera panned away, catching Zach driving forward, dipping his head, and using his shoulder to knock Radek off balance. The impact sent Radek stumbling to his knees, the rock slipping from his grasp. Zach barely stopped himself from crashing into the wall.

"That could have been nasty," Dotty said, looking up at Zach gratefully.

"I wasn't concerned about his safety," Zach replied, a touch defensively.

"No, I meant you. If you hadn't stopped before hitting the wall."

Zach blushed again and muttered something Dotty didn't catch.

Warren took back his phone and grinned. "Well done, mate. That was a brave thing you did. Another moment and …"

“That’s enough,” Keya cut in as she approached, tucking a manila folder into Dotty’s bag and handing it to her. “It’s clear Zach was Dotty’s knight in shining armour today.”

“Does that make me the damsel in distress?” Dotty asked, but she smiled warmly at Zach as she said it.

Zach returned the smile, then lowered his head toward hers. Her breath caught as their eyes locked, her chest tightening in anticipation.

Then his lips brushed against hers. Warm. Gentle.

“Ugh,” Warren groaned, breaking the spell.

Zach lingered for a moment longer before pulling away, his gaze still holding hers, a slow, conspiratorial smile forming.

Keya cleared her throat. “The ambulance is here.”

CHAPTER FORTY-FOUR

KEYA

Keya exhaled in relief as one of the paramedics finally turned their attention to Dotty.

Of course, they had been right to prioritise Dr Marston, carefully carrying, rather than pushing, the wheeled stretcher over the uneven ground to reach him.

When they returned, wheeling him the last stretch, they stopped briefly beside Zach's black Jeep, where Dotty was still sitting on the back seat, facing out through the open door.

Dr Marston slowly turned his head, offering Dotty a weak smile.

"Sorry," he mouthed, although Keya had no idea what he thought he needed to apologise for.

"Thank you," he added weakly.

Was he speaking to Dotty again or including her and Zach?

Dotty gave him a reassuring look and said gently, "I'm just glad you're all right."

The paramedics wheeled him towards the ambulance. Once his stretcher was lifted inside, one of them returned to check on Dotty.

They shone a light in her eyes and took her pulse.

"She can't put any weight on her ankle," Zach said.

"Did you fall?" the paramedic asked.

"Yes, I caught my foot."

"It was stuck in a hole," Keya added.

"Did you hear or feel a pop or snap?" the paramedic enquired. "And can you move your foot or wiggle your toes?"

"I didn't hear anything, but then I was more focused on …" She didn't finish, but quickly added, “But yes, I can move my foot.” She lifted it slightly and rotated her booted ankle. “And I think I can wiggle my toes.”

“Your boot will have helped stabilise it. I don’t want to remove it here and risk causing more swelling, but you need to come to the hospital with us.”

“Which hospital?” Keya asked.

“Cheltenham,” the paramedic replied before heading back to the ambulance.

As he returned with a wheelchair, Lynn joined them.

Warren remained by the police car, keeping a watchful eye on Radek.

“Everything all right?” Lynn asked.

“Dotty and Dr Marston are going to Cheltenham Hospital,” Keya replied.

“And I’ll follow them there,” Zach said firmly.

Lynn glanced around. “Someone needs to drive Radek’s car back to the station.”

"Excuse me," the paramedic said, manoeuvring the wheelchair beside the open car door.

They stepped aside as he helped Dotty into it.

"I'll drive Radek's car back," Keya volunteered.

"Thank you," Lynn said. "I appreciate that. Warren and I will take Radek in, and we still have Declan Reid to interview when we get back. At least now we're only questioning him about the stolen comic annuals, not Helen's death. Assuming Radek did kill her."

"He admitted as much," Dotty called as the paramedic wheeled her toward the ambulance. "And you should look into Pete Reynolds' death, too."

Lynn frowned. "We already did that. Does Dotty think Radek was involved?"

"I don't know," Keya admitted. "But if you need to question her, can it wait until after she's been treated?"

"Yes, of course," Lynn agreed. Then, glancing toward the Mercedes, she added, "And we need to find the car keys."

As the ambulance pulled away, Keya walked over to Radek's car. She was relieved to find the keys still in the ignition.

"The keys are here," she called to Lynn, who was approaching Warren.

"Good. Safe drive, and be careful. That car will be a lot quicker than your Polo."

Keya drove Radek's car carefully back to Cirencester and parked at the rear of the police station.

She wasn't sure yet whether it would be classified as a crime scene, but she might as well examine it in case there was any evidence linking Radek to Helen Fletcher's death.

But first, she needed to log it, and then she'd check if Sujin was still in his workroom. He had mentioned he would be starting the day at Cirencester but might be called out to police headquarters in Gloucester.

As she walked round the side of the modern

stone-clad building, she wondered about those at headquarters.

Would the murder squad swoop in now that Lynn and Warren, with her, Dotty, and Zach's help, had arrested the man they believed had killed Helen Fletcher, and possibly linked him to another death?

Probably not, she thought, as she stepped into the front reception area. There wouldn't be much glory in interviewing a man Warren had already arrested, and proving Radek had anything to do with Pete's death would likely be slow and difficult.

No, this was a win for Lynn and her team.

"Hi, Keya," the duty sergeant greeted her. "Inspector Lockwood said to expect you. Here's your pass."

He handed her a lanyard with her name already printed on it. She hoisted the blue strap over her head.

"Do you want me to log the suspect's car?" asked the sergeant.

"Thanks, but I'll do that. I also need to examine it," she smiled back at the uniformed officer.

He buzzed her through, and she opened the inner door leading to a ground floor corridor. The familiar blue nylon carpet had been replaced with a neutral grey one, and the lack of scuff marks on the walls suggested they had recently been repainted.

She passed the small kitchenette and entered her old team room. The previous inspector's office partition had been removed, incorporating the space into the main room. Like the corridor, it had a new grey carpet and fresh off-white walls.

Lynn and Warren were sitting at the far end, while two uniformed officers Keya didn't recognise worked at desks near the door. Lynn gestured for her to come over, and as she crossed the office, the two young officers regarded her curiously.

She had only been gone a few months, but already there were faces she didn't recognise, and people who didn't know her just as she didn't know them.

"We can't interview Radek straight away," Lynn said. "We thought it best to contact Matthew

Henshaw, and he's arranged for a solicitor. So in the meantime, we'll speak to Declan Reid. Hopefully, he just admits to the theft, and we can charge and release him. I don't have time to waste on a petty thief, not when the other case is far from being resolved."

"Oh, I thought now that Radek is in custody, everything would soon be tied up. I know Dotty suggested you also look into Pete Reynolds' death, but will that take long?"

"I'm not sure everything is as neat and tidy as we think," Lynn admitted. "Radek was muttering about treasure, about Matthew and Athena. I wish Dotty were here. She might know how it all fits together."

"Her injuries aren't life threatening, so hopefully she won't have to stay in the hospital overnight. She'll need to rest, but maybe she can enlighten us all tomorrow."

Lynn stood up. "Let's hope so. Come on, Warren. Let's get this interview over with." Turning back to Keya she asked, "Are you visiting Sujin?"

"Yes, and then I thought I'd examine the Mercedes, just to be thorough."

"Thank you. It all helps bring this case to a conclusion."

CHAPTER FORTY-FIVE

DOTTY

"I hope you don't mind meeting in the cafe rather than at the police station," Lynn said.

"At least there's cake," Warren added, eyeing up the Victoria sponge in the centre of the table.

It was late on Friday afternoon and the end of a long and eventful week. Dotty was happy to be meeting at the Waterwheel Cafe.

After Zach had forced her to take Wednesday and Thursday off, following the incident at the derelict house, she had spent much of the day catching up with work and appreciated not having to drive to Cirencester.

“I’ve already had a long discussion with Matthew Henshaw, and I appreciate him agreeing to speak to us all today.” Lynn glanced at Matthew, who seemed more stooped and frail than when Dotty had last seen him. He’d leaned on Imogen earlier as they’d made their way steadily across the cafe’s flagstone floor.

“I’m also grateful to Dr Marston for joining us, although I’m not sure he should have discharged himself from hospital.” Lynn regarded Hugo steadily. The right side of his face was swollen and bruised, and partially obscured by a thick wad of white gauze dressing.

“I wouldn’t miss this, or the food,” he said, also eyeing the cake with interest.

“And Laura and Beth, thank you for coming. As I mentioned, this is an informal discussion, and nothing said here will be documented in the formal investigation. If I need to look further into anything, I’ll conduct separate interviews.”

“Whose coffees are these?” Keya asked as she set a round black tray on the table. She passed mugs to Imogen, Zach, and Lynn. Everyone else had opted for tea.

Finally, once everyone was settled with their hot drinks and, for those who wanted it, a slice of golden Victoria sponge, Matthew cleared his throat.

Dotty took a bite of cake, then licked her fingers. Delicious.

"Matthew has asked to speak first and for you to refrain from asking questions. Some parts of his story are painful to tell, and there are others he is not proud of. While each of you will form your own opinions, he asks that you don't judge him too harshly."

Dotty sat back, and Zach reached for her hand, squeezing it reassuringly.

Matthew began.

"This all started in Saxony, in eastern Germany, in 1946, after the end of the Second World War. I was attached to a small unit of British soldiers taking inventory of abandoned wartime equipment."

Matthew hesitated for a moment, then continued, his voice steady.

"You see, I am not actually English. I was born Anton Vašek in 1928 in western Czechoslovakia. My family lived modestly, but they encouraged my fascination with languages. That led me, towards the end of the war, into contact first with German, and then with British soldiers."

A sharp intake of breath passed around the table.

Imogen gasped. "Grandad!" she exclaimed.

But Matthew held up his hand, his gaze shifting to Laura.

"Your grandfather gave me the nickname 'The Little Owl,' and the rest of the unit adopted it. I became their mascot, perhaps even a symbol of someone they had freed from the Nazi regime. When the Russians advanced, they agreed to take me back to England."

Dotty stared at Matthew, fascinated. She had so many questions, but for now, she'd respect Matthew's request and let him continue.

"We had just arrived at an abandoned manor house near Leipzig when the unit received orders to return home and hand over any German equipment or valuables to the Russians. But inside the manor, we discovered a stash of Nazi treasures. The officers must have fled, leaving it behind. We didn't want to leave it for the Russians, knowing it would likely vanish. But could we take it?"

He paused before continuing. "Lieutenant Francis sent some of the unit out, and they returned with two U.S. Army trucks and an Austin Tilly. We loaded most of the treasure into the trucks and the unit's own vehicles. The night before we were due to leave, we discussed what to do about the house itself, its contents, and what would happen once the Russians arrived."

Matthew exhaled slowly, running his hands over his face.

"We couldn't leave it all there. Some of the men picked out items for themselves, and I saw the lieutenant tuck away a gold chalice. I helped Sergeant Henshaw wrap paintings and pack several boxes of smaller, more fragile objects, which we loaded into his old Tilly. The following morning, the others climbed into their vehicles, and I got in beside Sergeant Henshaw. We set off, but the Tilly developed a puncture, so we sent the others on ahead."

Dotty was fascinated to finally learn the full story.

"When we were ready," Matthew continued, "I suggested a shortcut I had taken with Pete a few days earlier. I never saw the shooter. One moment, the sergeant was whistling as he drove, and the next, he slumped over the steering wheel, the vehicle swerving across the road. I had to act fast. I shoved him aside and kept driving until I reached an abandoned farmhouse. Only then did I realise he was dead."

He looked round the table, but most faces remained blank, absorbing the story.

"I didn't know what to do. If someone found us, they'd assume I had killed the sergeant, and I couldn't continue on my own without being accused of theft. But waiting for the Russians, after all the reports we'd heard of their brutal treatment of both civilians and soldiers, was not an option. Nor was staying in eastern Germany or returning to Czechoslovakia. So I did the only thing I could think of.

"I undressed the sergeant and put on his uniform. It was too big for me, but I tightened his belt and tucked in his shirt. And poor Sergeant Henshaw… I left his body in a barn in Saxony. I'm not proud of that, but his name lived on when I took his identity. I joined another British convoy heading west. No one questioned me, and before long, I found myself on a ship to England. I followed other units to London and demobbed as Matthew Henshaw."

Dr Hugo couldn't restrain himself. He leaned forward and asked, "And the treasure?"

Matthew sighed. "This is where my actions are harder to defend. But it wasn't the stolen Nazi loot. The sergeant and I had been taking back objects from the manor house on behalf of the unit. At first, I didn't know what to do with them. I stored them, intending to find the others. But then I realised I couldn't do that. I was now Matthew Henshaw. If I went to them, they'd ask questions about what had happened, and why I'd taken Matt's name. They might even think I'd killed him."

He shuddered. "And if they had handed me over to the authorities? I was terrified. In London, I had a chance at a new life. Back home in Czechoslovakia, those I left behind were trapped under Soviet rule. What would any of you have done?"

"I'd have handed over the treasure," declared Hugo, pushing at the white padding on the side of his head.

"I don't know," Zach admitted. "Things were different back then."

Matthew nodded. "They certainly were. But if you were willing to work hard, there were opportunities. To get started, I discreetly sold a couple of paintings, which gave me enough money to travel to France and buy soap and coffee. I sold those in London for a profit. Then I repeated the process, trading bicycle parts and stockings from Belgium and the Netherlands. I relied on my language skills, learned how to spot trouble, and built a successful trading business."

"As Matthew Henshaw," Laura commented.

"Yes. And your grandfather eventually tracked me down, although I avoided meeting him in person. I would have loved to attend the unit reunion, but it was too risky. Still, he sent me a tiny gold owl, which I have kept."

Matthew reached into his pocket and removed a small golden owl pendant. One eye was red, the other orange, and its wings were slightly raised, as if poised for flight.

Hugo unfurled his hand, but Beth was quicker, reaching for the pendant first and cradling it in her palm.

Imogen tilted her head. “Is that why your company is called Athena Trading?”

“Yes,” Matthew confirmed. “In Greek mythology, Athena was the goddess of wisdom, strategy, and warfare. One of her symbols was the owl.”

Beth smiled as she studied the pendant. “So many owls.”

“And now,” Dotty said, “we finally know the truth.”

“May I?” Hugo asked, reaching for the owl.

Beth let it drop into his open hand.

“Thank you for telling us all this, although I can’t help wondering if opening up earlier would have saved a lot of trouble,” Dotty remarked.

Lynn raised her eyebrows but didn’t interrupt.

"Quite possibly, but when?" Matthew asked. "At the beginning, when I was a lonely immigrant with an assumed identity? Later, when I had a fledgling business to protect? Or when I moved to the Cotswolds, with a successful business and a reputation to uphold?"

"When you knew Helen had found her father's trunk of wartime memorabilia. Or when Pete Reynolds approached you, recognising who you really were," Dotty reasoned.

Lynn smiled encouragingly but remained silent.

"Pete did approach you, didn't he?" Dotty pressed.

Matthew hesitated, and then nodded. "Yes, and you're right, I should have been more open. But I was busy in the lead-up to Christmas. That's why I invited him to the veterans' dinner. Such a shame about his accident."

Dotty glanced at Lynn, who gave her a perceptible nod.

"You see, I'm not sure it was an accident," Dotty said quietly.

"But what else could it have been?" Matthew protested, his brow furrowing.

"I think Radek knew Pete recognised you as the unit's interpreter. Pete would have remembered that you and Sergeant Henshaw travelled together, and it wouldn't have been difficult for him to piece the rest together. Did Radek say anything to you?" Dotty asked.

"Not directly, but he had a way of not saying what he thought. He kept his thoughts close, which I suppose was a consequence of growing up in East Germany."

"You knew that? You knew who and what he was?" Dotty pressed.

"Not at first, although it was immediately clear he wasn't a native Czech, despite his efforts to blend in at the social club. But I recognised something in him. A desperation, a sense of being lost. The quick sharp reactions of a frightened animal with something to hide. Initially he did the jobs nobody else wanted.

"I suppose he proved his worth and loyalty to me. Slowly, I realised he was German, but it was many years before I discovered he'd been recruited by the Stasi as a child. But by then, I knew the man, and I accepted him for what he had become."

Lynn's voice remained steady as she said, "I can confirm we are investigating Radek for the death of Peter Reynolds."

CHAPTER FORTY-SIX

KEYA

"And for the murder of Helen Fletcher, and the attempted murders of Dr Marston and Dotty?" Keya asked, her eyes widening as she looked across the cafe table at Lynn.

Lynn cut into her slice of Victoria sponge and lifted a piece to her mouth before replying. "Yes, we're looking into all of those."

"I presume Radek saw Helen as a threat, just as Pete had been?" Keya questioned.

"But a threat to whom?" Matthew asked, his voice edged with uncertainty.

Dotty turned to him. "To you and everything you've built. And if people discovered who you really were, he might have feared they'd also uncover who and what he was. He talked about your reputation and I think he was prepared to protect it, and by default his own, by whatever means necessary."

"But it wasn't necessary to harm those people," Matthew protested. He shook his head. "I should have realised what he was capable of."

Imogen spoke up. "Grandad, you can't blame yourself for what he did."

Matthew sighed. "Perhaps if I had seen what was happening sooner, instead of focusing so much on my legacy, and on trying to give back to those who'd been persecuted by war, and lost all their possessions."

Lynn shook her head. "We all have to be responsible for our own actions. Although I think Radek has a rather twisted view of reality."

That would explain a lot, Keya thought. She said, "So on the Saturday of Helen's death, Radek arrived at The Owl's Nook around four o'clock and parked his car outside?"

Lynn nodded. “The arrival of his car has been confirmed but nobody saw him enter the bookshop, and we haven’t found any witnesses who saw him inside with Helen that afternoon. So we can only speculate about what happened.” She glanced at Dotty. “I think you have the best theory.”

Dotty took a breath. “Radek might have thought he’d solved his problem when Pete fell down the stairs and later died, believing he could continue protecting both Matthew and himself. But I think he later found out that Pete and Helen had been discussing the war, and her father, and that worried him. Then, at Dr Marston’s event the week before Helen died, I believe two key things happened.”

“First, Matthew let slip that he had personally seen looted treasures during the war and now wanted to set things right, supporting organisations working to recover what had been lost. That led him to meet with Hugo to discuss his charitable donations.”

“That’s true,” Matthew acknowledged. “I’d been considering doing something for a while, but I wasn’t sure what until I heard Dr Marston speak.”

Dotty nodded. "Which is why Radek might have started worrying about what you and Dr Marston might uncover. It wasn't just about the money, or you giving it away, it was about what else might come to light."

"Was that one incident or two?" Keya asked.

"That was the first. The second was that Helen told Matthew about finding a trunk of her father's things. She mentioned Saxony, treasure, and a young interpreter. She was also wearing the owl pendant that had belonged to her father.

"Radek knew about Deerpark House, so I assume he also knew about the treasure. He must have been worried about what the trunk would reveal. But did he understand the pendant's true significance? And Matthew, did you know that Helen's father had been the commanding officer of The Little Owl's unit?"

Matthew's face lit up. "I couldn't believe it. Here was the link to my past that I had been searching for. And then, when I noticed the pendant Helen was wearing round her neck, I couldn't wait to speak to her properly about her father and the unit. I told Radek as much as we drove home."

Dotty nodded. "And that's when Radek sensed danger. Having already dealt with one former member of your wartime unit, you'd now found the family of another. Who knows what you would have told Helen if you'd had the chance to sit down with her? I suspect you'd have finally come clean about your true identity."

"Quite possibly," Matthew admitted.

"So Radek saw Helen as a major threat, and in his mind, there was only one way to deal with her," Dotty concluded.

"Which is why he went to The Owl's Nook?" Keya prompted.

Lynn nodded. "That's the theory we're working on, although despite extensive questioning, Radek hasn't admitted to anything. And I'm not sure he ever will."

Matthew exhaled. "He'd have been subjected to very harsh interrogation techniques as a child. If he doesn't want to talk, I doubt you'll get anything out of him."

Lynn sighed. "We may never know exactly what he and Helen discussed. He might have enquired about her father's wartime possessions under the guise of speaking on your behalf, trying to gauge what she knew. The discussion may have become heated, or he might have simply decided Helen needed to be silenced. But at some point, he picked up the wooden owl and struck her with it. Attacking people with a blow to the head seemed to be his method of choice, possibly learned during his Stasi training."

Dr Marston grimaced, touching the bandage on his head. "Don't I know it."

Dotty shivered.

Keya glanced at her with understanding. If she and Zach had been a few minutes later… but she didn't want to dwell on that thought.

Instead, she brought them back to the facts. "We've matched a partial print on the wooden owl to Radek."

The group was silent until Laura finally spoke. "I'd like to thank you all for helping uncover the truth about Mum's death. And I'm sorry that some of you were hurt in the process." She looked at Dr Marston and Dotty.

Matthew bowed his head. Then he looked up and said, “No, I should be the one thanking you all and apologising for not acting sooner. I know it’s not much, but I would like to set up one of my new charities in Lieutenant Francis’ name, if you think that’s appropriate.” He looked at Laura.

Laura smiled. “I think he would have preferred you to remember his entire unit, including the young interpreter.”

Beth, quiet until now, spoke up. “Why not call it The Little Owls?”

“That’s a lovely idea. And would you like to sit on the board?” Matthew asked.

Beth’s eyes widened. “Me?” She looked at her mother.

Laura smiled. “I think that’s a fabulous idea.”

Beth hesitated, before nodding. Then she said, “I propose the logo be based on the owl pendants.”

“Seconded,” Imogen responded.

Matthew gave a small nod of approval.

“Then it’s settled. One of the charities will be

called The Little Owls, and its logo will be based on the owl pendants."

CHAPTER FORTY-SEVEN

DOTTY

"Lot 28. A 1987 hardcover special deluxe edition of the *Steel Sentinels* annual, a 1981 annual featuring Captain Crucible's debut, and three more early editions," Zach announced.

He was seated on a raised platform in the former aircraft hangar that currently housed Cirencester Auctioneers.

To his left, Amanda tapped a key on her computer keyboard, and the screen behind them displayed images of the collection of comic annuals.

Dotty watched as the bidding climbed. She was pleased they had included the items in the auction as it would give everyone closure. Laura had generously agreed to split the proceeds with Declan, reasoning that they would never have known the true value of the comics without him.

"£3,000," called Zach, and the figure on the screen updated behind them.

Dotty spotted Laura and Beth sitting together on an old purple sofa, facing the auctioneer's rostrum.

"£3,050. £3,100." The bids continued to creep up via the internet.

They slowed after reaching £4,000. Zach raised his gavel at £4,250 and declared, "This is your final warning."

When no more bids were placed, he brought the gavel down. "Sold for £4,250."

In the audience, Laura and Beth high-fived each other, clearly delighted with the outcome.

The auction continued for another half an hour before Zach announced, "Ladies and gentlemen, we'll now take a ten-minute break before starting the paintings and picture section."

Dotty caught Laura and Beth exchanging excited glances.

The Josef Stoitzner painting had been included as one of the star lots, and from the buzz in the room and the steady stream of people arriving through the front doors, it was clearly proving popular.

Clara appeared, carrying tea for Dotty and coffee for Amanda and Zach. "That was a great start," she said, her eyes bright with enthusiasm. Placing a property brochure in front of Amanda, she added, "This looks fascinating, but you've got a lot of work to do."

Dotty glanced at the brochure and caught her breath.

"What's the matter?" Amanda asked.

"That house. Are you buying it?"

"Yes. Although Clara's right. It does need loads of work, but the views are incredible."

They weren't what stood out in Dotty's mind from her visit to Deerfield House.

"I'll change the name, since there aren't any deer," Amanda continued. "What do you think about Beacon Hill, Cotswolds View, or High Ridge Hall?"

Dotty didn't mind what Amanda called it, as long as she changed its name. Hopefully, once the renovations were complete, it wouldn't bear any resemblance to the derelict property where she had nearly lost her life.

Zach drained his mug of coffee and said, "Shall we continue?"

"Marion and I both have phone bidders for the Stoitzner painting," Clara reminded him.

As a late addition to the auction, the Josef Stoitzner painting was at the end of the paintings and picture section. Clara had created its own insert for the brochure, and as its image appeared on the screen behind the rostrum, people in the crowded auction room reached for their copies.

Zach began, "Lot 139. A Josef Stoitzner landscape painting of Austria, circa 1930. Originally part of a set of three, rescued after the Second World War from a manor in East Germany. I've had several pre-auction bids for this attractive and historically significant painting, so I will be starting the bidding at £37,000."

Several people gasped, and Dotty saw Beth grab her mother's arm. But Dotty needed to focus on her screen and the internet bidding.

The price rose rapidly to £46,000 before stalling. Zach glanced at Marion and Clara, who were both speaking quietly to clients on their phones.

Marion nodded, and Zach continued. "£46,500… £47,000, on the internet."

Marion nodded again.

The game continued, with bidding from both Marion's client and an online bidder driving the price past £50,000. At this point, Clara put her phone down.

At £53,500, after another bid from Marion's client, the online bidding stopped.

Zach looked round the room. "Any advance on £53,500?"

When no one responded, he checked the internet for a final time before bringing the gavel down. "Sold."

Dotty smiled at Marion and nodded. On her green

bidding sheet, she ticked Phone Bidder and wrote the name Matthew Henshaw.

He had wanted to keep his involvement anonymous, but he had confided in Dotty that, after seeking Hugo's advice, he would be donating the painting to the Commission for Looted Art in Europe.

Hugo had already contacted the only living descendant of Friedrich Albrecht, the painting's original owner. She was a woman in her sixties, and they had agreed that the Commission should place the painting in the Leopold Museum in Vienna.

Matthew had also commissioned Hugo to find and approach the owners of the other two paintings in the set, offering to buy them so they could be reunited and displayed together.

Hugo was excited about the commission and the opportunity to work with Imogen to realise Matthew's charitable aspirations. In addition, he had recently discovered that Matthew had kept much of the original treasure from Deerfield House and suggested it be donated to the German Lost Art Foundation.

"And that concludes the paintings and picture section. We'll take a fifteen-minute break before we start with the furniture," Zach announced, before switching off his microphone.

Laura and Beth stood and made their way towards the platform.

Dotty also rose and stretched her arms before descending the steps to meet them.

"That was so exciting," Beth said, her eyes wide and bright.

"Yes, it was," Laura agreed. "And it was incredibly generous of Pete to leave Beth the painting."

Dotty smiled and asked, "Do you know what you're going to do with the money?"

Beth nodded. "I'd like to study Cultural Heritage and Museum Studies at Leicester or University College London. Or, if I do well enough in my A Levels, an MA in Art History at Cambridge."

"But before that," Laura confided, looking warmly at her daughter, "we're planning a trip to Europe this summer."

"Yes," Beth added brightly. "I want to visit Vienna, Leipzig, and Berlin…"

"And learn more about the Second World War," Laura finished.

Beth nodded more seriously. "Yes."

"That sounds like an excellent idea," agreed Dotty. "I hope you enjoy it."

"So you see," said Dotty, "we no longer have the option of using Cirencester Auctioneers' premises for future auctions. Amanda is completing the sale of her unit this Friday."

She glanced round the auction office.

Clara and Marion had left early so she, Zach, Gilly, Aunt Beanie, and Marmaduke could hold a meeting about Akemans' future.

"But we can't move the stalls back into the antique centre," Gilly protested. "Another piece of plaster fell down this morning. In fact, more stallholders are asking to move into the auction space."

"And what are we going to do when the work starts?" enquired Aunt Beanie.

"If," Marmaduke muttered, but everyone ignored him.

"We've agreed on a staged approach with the contractor," Zach explained. "The first step will be to clear out the storerooms. Then we'll redecorate and improve the lighting in them so we can use them for May's auction."

Dotty crossed her fingers, hoping the work would be completed in time. She still had no idea where they would store the auction items that had already been delivered, but Zach had assured her the contractor would work around them.

"Once that's complete, we can use the space for antique stalls while we begin the major works in the auction house and antique centre. I won't pretend there won't be any disruptions, but we'll do our best to keep them to a minimum," Zach reassured them.

"Well, I think you've done an amazing job sorting this out so quickly, and I'm very excited to see how the premises will look when you've finished," Aunt Beanie said approvingly. "And on that note, as we have a quorum of the board, I would like to propose Zach as Akemans' new Managing Director."

"I second that," Gilly confirmed.

"Marmaduke," growled Aunt Beanie.

Her brother folded his arms and grunted, "Agreed."

"Motion passed," Aunt Beanie declared. "Zach is officially the new Managing Director, and we look forward to seeing his plans for rejuvenating the business."

Dotty smiled and reached for Zach's hand, squeezing it supportively.

"Congratulations," she murmured in his ear.

He turned and kissed her on the cheek. "Thank you. I can't wait for us to start working together."

A WICKET OF LIES

Summer is in full swing in the Cotswolds — but not everyone is playing fair.

Keya is thrilled to be batting for the Coln Akeman Larks in a village cricket festival final. Dotty? Not so much. She's much happier preparing the afternoon tea than facing fast bowlers.

But when an unexpected injury puts Dotty on the sidelines and a reluctant newcomer steps in, no one expects the substitute to end up dead.

At first it looks like a tragic accident, but as lies unravel and suspicions grow, it's clear someone isn't playing by the rules.

As Dotty tries to uncover the truth behind the lies swirling around the cricket pitch, she's also facing uncertainty in her personal life. Can she let go of her doubts and commit to a future with Zach?

With a murder to solve and the game underway, can Dotty, Keya, and their unlikely team of village cricketers spot the real villain before someone else gets bowled out?

Keep your eye on the ball and uncover the truth in A Wicket of Lies today!

Inheritance and Intrigue in the Cotswolds

Grappling with self-doubt after the death of her husband, Marcus, Georgina Carey begins to rebuild her life—one mystery at a time.

In this **FREE prequel**, Georgina discovers a sapphire ring in Marcus' safe. Determined to return it, she soon finds herself caught between two women—both claiming it as their own.

As tensions rise and betrayals come to light, she unearths secrets tied to an unsolved death.

Can she expose the truth before the past tears a family apart?

Read Inheritance and Intrigue in the Cotswolds for FREE

If you enjoyed this book, please tell someone you know. And for those people you don't know, leave a review to help them decide whether or not to read it.

Leave a review on Amazon

For more information visit VictoriaTait.com

UNTITLED

Printed in Great Britain
by Amazon

62476714R00238